Dear parents,

¡Hola! We are proud to present this book for you and your child to read and explore together. This book is a great step for emerging readers who are ready to move past board books and picture books and into books with chapters. The two stories featured in this book contain four short chapters each. The chapters are the perfect length for reading to your child in one sitting before bed, while waiting in the doctor's office, or any time of day. Your child is sure to enjoy this "big kid" book featuring the illustrated adventures of their friend Dora!

¡Vámonos! Let's go! And happy reading!

Dora's Fantastic Tales

Based on the TV series *Dora the Explorer*™ as seen on Nick Jr.™

DISCARD

3 1350 00309 8938

SIMON SPOTLIGHT/NICKELODEON

An imprint of Simon & Schuster Children's Publishing Division

1230 Avenue of the Americas, New York, New York 10020

© 2009 Viacom International Inc. All rights reserved. English language translation copyright © 2011 by Viacom International Inc. All rights reserved. NICKELODEON, NICK JR., *Dora the Explorer*, and all related titles, logos, and characters are trademarks of Viacom International Inc. Originally published in France in 2009 by Albin Michel, S.A. as *Dora magicienne*. First Simon Spotlight edition published 2011. All rights reserved, including the right of reproduction in whole or in part in any form. SIMON SPOTLIGHT and colophon are registered trademarks of Simon & Schuster, Inc. For information about special discounts for bulk purchases, please contact Simon & Schuster Special Sales at 1-866-506-1949 or business@simonandschuster.com.

Manufactured in China 1211 SCP

10 9 8 7 6 5 4 3

ISBN 978-1-4424-3311-3

nickelodeon™

DORA the EXPLORER™

Dora's Fantastic Tales

adapted by Valérie Videau
based on the screenplays "The Big Red Chicken's Magic Show"
and "Isa's Unicorn Flowers" written by Rosemary Contreras

Simon Spotlight/Nickelodeon
New York London Toronto Sydney

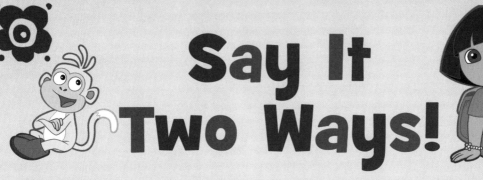

Say It Two Ways!

¡Hola! Are you ready for an adventure? I need your help on my adventures, and I need your help using English *and* Spanish words too! Say it two ways with me!

Spanish	English
Abre, puerta	Open, door
Crezcan, flores	Grow, flowers
Fantástico	Fantastic
Gracias	Thank you
Hola	Hello
Mami	Mommy
Mira	Look

Spanish	English
No te preocupes	Don't worry
¿Que?	What?
Qué lindas	How pretty
Sí	Yes
Vámonos	Let's go
Uno	One
Dos	Two
Tres	Three
Cuatro	Four
Cinco	Five
Seis	Six
Siete	Seven

1

The Magic Show

Chapter 1
The Magic Wand

Today is a very special day. The Big Red Chicken is going to be a magician in his very own magic show! Dora and Boots can't wait to see the magic show. Would you like to see the Big Red Chicken's magic tricks? Great!

Dora and Boots are waiting for the Big Red Chicken to come out on stage. They need to call him. Will you help? Say "Big Red Chicken." One more time. "Big Red Chicken."

There he is! He's wearing a cape and a black top hat. He has a magic wand to help him do his tricks.

"Welcome to my magic show," announces the Big Red Chicken. "For my first trick I'm going to make a bunny appear!"

The Big Red Chicken places his top hat on a table. He waves his magic wand over the hat. But no bunny appears.

"I forgot the magic word!" the Big Red Chicken exclaims.

Dora and Boots want to help the Big Red Chicken remember the magic word.

"Is it abra-spaghetti?" asks the Big Red Chicken.

"Try again," says Dora.

"Is it abra-hamburger?" asks the Big Red Chicken.

"No, that's silly," says Boots.

Do you know what the magic word is? *¡Sí!* It's abracadabra.

"Oh, yeah!" says the Big Red Chicken.

The Big Red Chicken waves his magic wand over the hat. He says the magic word. Look! A bunny wearing a bow tie is hopping out of the hat!

"It worked! It worked!" cries the Big Red Chicken.

"Great trick!" says Dora.

The Big Red Chicken raises his magic wand. "For my next trick I'm going to make the bunny disappear." But the wand slips out of his hand. The wand soars through the air and lands right in the bunny's paws. The bunny waves the magic wand and *poof!* He disappears! And . . . something else happens!

"Look!" says Boots. "The Big Red Chicken isn't big anymore."

"He's wearing the bunny's bow tie, and he became small like the bunny," says Dora.

"I really want to be big again," the Big Red Chicken groans. "I need to find my magic wand."

Will you help Dora and Boots find the bunny with the magic wand? *¡Fantástico!*

"The bunny must have gone back to Magic

Land through the hat," says Boots.

"Let's go there and find him," says Dora.

To get to Magic Land, Dora and Boots need to say "abracadabra." Say it with them.

"Abracadabra!" shout Dora and Boots.

Chapter 2
The Queen
of Hearts

Great job! Dora, Boots, and the Big Red Chicken are in Magic Land!

"How are we going to find the bunny, Dora?" asks the Big Red Chicken.

"Who do we ask for help when we don't know which way to go?" asks Dora. "Map! *¡Sí!*"

Map pops out of Backpack. Map knows where to find the bunny with the magic wand. "The bunny is at Bunny Hill," says Map.

"But how do we get there?" asks Boots.

"First you have to go through the Card Castle," Map explains. "Then past the Magic Cup Forest. And that's how you get to Bunny Hill!"

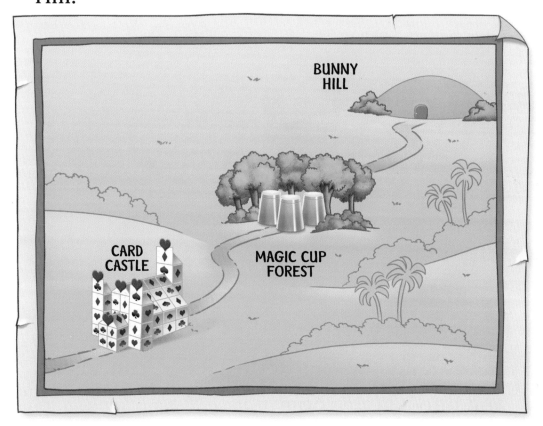

"Thanks, Map!" says Dora. "So first we need to find the castle."

Do you see a castle made out of cards? Yeah, at the top of that hill!

"All we have to do is follow the path up the hill," explains Dora. "*¡Vámonos!* Let's go!"

When they arrive at the Card Castle, Dora, Boots, and the Big Red Chicken run inside and into a large room.

"Wow!" exclaims Boots. "Look at all the cards."

Dora, Boots, and the Big Red Chicken look all around, but there is no door out of the room. "How will we get through the castle if there is no door?" asks the Big Red Chicken.

All of a sudden the Queen of Hearts appears.

"*Hola*, Dora! *Hola*, Boots! *Hola*, Big Red Chicken!" she greets them. "To get through my castle you must do a card trick."

"I'm good at card tricks," says the Big Red Chicken.

The Queen of Hearts holds out a deck of cards. "Pick a card, any card," she tells them.

The Big Red Chicken takes a card and gives it to Dora. It's the seven of hearts.

"Now to do this trick," says the Queen of Hearts, "you have to remember the number of hearts on the card before I make them disappear. Then you have to find them all to fill in the card."

The queen waves her magic scepter and the card goes blank. How many hearts were on the card? Seven! *¡Sí!*

"Now we have to find the seven red hearts to fill the card," says Dora.

Do you see seven red hearts in the room? Count them in Spanish with Dora and Boots. *Uno. Dos. Tres. Cuatro. Cinco. Seis. Siete.* Seven hearts—you found them all!

Great job! Thanks to you, Dora, Boots, and the Big Red Chicken decorated the blank card with the seven hearts and the Queen of Hearts allowed them through her beautiful castle!

Chapter 3
Magic Backpack!

Now that Dora, Boots, and the Big Red Chicken have made it through the Card Castle, they are on their way to the Magic Cup Forest.

Do you see the Magic Cup Forest? Yes! It's up ahead.

But when Dora, Boots, and the Big Red Chicken run down the path, the Big Red Chicken falls into a hole.

"*Bawk! Bawk!* Help! Help!" he cries.

Boots stretches down to pull the Big Red Chicken out of the hole, but his arm isn't long enough. "I can't reach him. We need something to get him out of the hole."

"I bet Backpack has something to help pull the Big Red Chicken out of that hole," says Dora.

Say "Backpack!"

Backpack pops up, ready to help. Do you see something that Dora can use to pull the Big Red Chicken out of the hole?

Smart thinking! Dora can use the rope!

Dora takes the rope, but when Boots looks at it, he frowns. "That rope is too short," he says.

"But this is a magic rope, Boots," Dora says. "We just have to say the magic word to make it really long."

Do you remember what the magic word is? Yeah! Abracadabra! Say it. In a flash the rope grows really long. Now Dora and Boots can use it to pull the Big Red Chicken out of the hole.

Chapter 4
Find the
Right Bunny

Dora, Boots, and the Big Red Chicken continue on their way to the Magic Cup Forest. But once they get there, they discover that the path is blocked by three giant cups.

"We have to get past these cups to get to Bunny Hill," says Boots.

"These are magic cups," says Dora. "There must be some trick to get them to move."

Then Dora and Boots hear someone calling to them.

"Look. It's my friend, Najim," says Dora. "He likes magic tricks, too. Maybe he can help us get past these cups."

Najim knows what kind of cups these are. "If you say the word 'cup,' these magic cups will wiggle."

Help Dora, Boots, and the Big Red Chicken. Say "cup."

"Look!" says the Big Red Chicken. "The cups are wiggling."

"That's right," says Najim. "And to make the cups move out of the way, we have to find the magic ball. There is a ball underneath one of the cups. When you see the ball peek out from underneath a cup, clap your hands together."

Will you clap with Dora and her friends? Great. Do you see a ball in the first cup? No. Do you see a ball in the second cup? No. What about the third cup? Do you see a ball in there? There it is! Clap your hands!

Great job! Thank you for helping find the magic ball. Now the cups have moved out of the way. The Big Red Chicken can find the bunny, and he can be big again.

"Hurry!" says the Big Red Chicken. "We're almost there."

But when the friends get to Bunny Hill, they don't see any bunnies.

"Where did the bunnies go?" asks the Big Red Chicken.

"I think the bunnies are *inside* the hill," says Dora. "We need to find a door."

Do you see a door? Yes! There's a purple door.

"Open, door!" commands the Big Red Chicken, but the door doesn't open.

"*¿Que?*" asks the door.

"This door speaks Spanish," says Dora. "We need to tell the door to open in Spanish. In English we say 'Open, door!' In Spanish we say '*¡Abre, puerta!*'"

Will you help Dora, Boots, and the Big Red Chicken open the door? Say "*¡Abre, puerta!*" The door is opening. Great job!

There are lots of bunnies inside Bunny Hill, and each bunny is wearing a bow tie except for one.

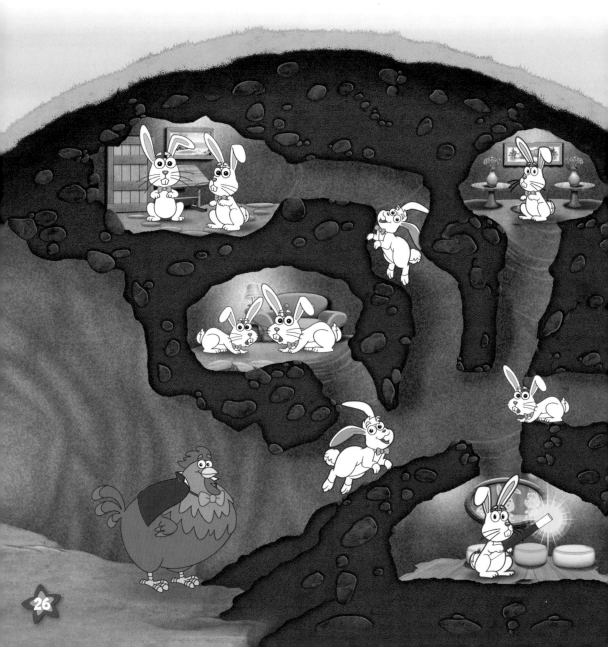

Do you see the bunny without a bow tie? That's the bunny that took the Big Red Chicken's magic wand.

"My wand!" cries the Big Red Chicken. He takes the wand back, and he returns the bunny's bow tie. Then the Big Red Chicken says the magic word, "Abracadabra."

The Big Red Chicken is big again!

"We did it!" shouts Dora.

Thank you for helping Dora, Boots, and the Big Red Chicken. They couldn't have done it without you! *¡Gracias!*

2

Unicorn Flowers

Chapter I
Hello, Unicornio!

It's a beautiful afternoon, and Dora and Isa are planting flowers in Dora's flower garden. There are so many different kinds of flowers. Dora's favorite are the pretty pink butterfly flowers in the shape of butterflies.

"I love sunny days, and I love planting flowers," says Isa.

"Me too," agrees Dora. "And you have so many different types of seeds, Isa."

"Yeah," says Isa, planting seeds from a new packet. "Like these special number seeds."

To get the number seeds to grow, Dora and Isa have to say "*¡Crezcan, flores!*" Grow, flowers! Will you say it with them? Great!

"*¡Mira!* The number seeds grew into number flowers," says Dora. "Let's count them in Spanish. *Uno, dos, tres, cuatro, cinco.*"

As Dora counts, Isa notices something very special up in the sky. "Look! A beautiful rainbow."

"And there's a unicorn at the bottom of it!" adds Dora.

The unicorn trots up to Dora and Isa. "*¡Hola!* My name is Unicornio. I like your unicorn flowers. They look just like my horn."

"Wow, they do!" says Dora.

"Unicorn flowers are my *mami's* favorite," Unicornio continues.

Dora has an idea. "Would you like some unicorn flowers to bring home to your *mami*?"

"Yes!" says Unicornio. "*Gracias*, Dora."

Dora ties some unicorn flowers into a necklace and places it around Unicornio's neck. When he gets home, he can give the flowers to his *mami*!

Isa has a question for their new friend. "How did you get here, Unicornio?"

"I rode down on that rainbow," says Unicornio.

But the rainbow is starting to fade away.

"I need to ride the rainbow home to the Unicorn Forest so I can give the unicorn flowers to my *mami*!" cries Unicornio.

"*No te preocupes*, Unicornio," says Dora. "Don't worry. We'll help you find the rainbow."

Who does Dora ask for help when she doesn't know which way to go? The Map, right! Say "Map!"

Map flies out of Backpack. "Dora and Isa need to find the Rainbow fast so that Unicornio can take the flowers home to his *mami*. I know how to get there fast.

"First you have to go past the Dragon's Cave, then over the Troll Bridge. And that's how you'll get to the Rainbow!"

RAINBOW

TROLL BRIDGE

DRAGON'S CAVE

"Thanks, Map!" says Dora.

"First we have to go to the Dragon's Cave.
¡Vámonos! Let's go!"

Chapter 2
Beware the Dragon

At first Dora, Isa, and Unicornio don't see the dragon when they reach the Dragon's Cave. But when they get closer they hear a loud roar as the dragon flies out of his cave.

"There's the dragon," says Unicornio. "And he's blocking our way!"

"How are we going to get past the dragon, Dora?" asks Isa.

As Dora is thinking, she sees her friend Mei from China.

"In China they have lots of dragon stories," explains Dora. "Maybe Mei knows what we can do."

Dora explains that they are trying to take Unicornio home to his *mami* and they need to get past the dragon.

Mei knows how to help. "There's a special dragon dance that dragons love. If we all do the dragon dance, he'll move out of the way."

Will you do the dragon dance with Dora and her friends? Great! Here's how you do it. First you have to wiggle your feet. Then you flap your arms. Now roar like a dragon. Wow! The dragon dance is working. The dragon is dancing out of the way!

"Thank you for helping us, Mei," says Dora.

"Yippee!" shouts Unicornio. "We made it past the Dragon's Cave."

"Where do we go next, Dora?" asks Isa.

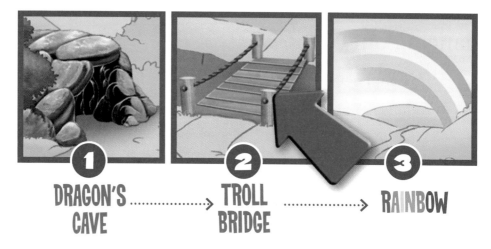

1 DRAGON'S CAVE ·············> 2 TROLL BRIDGE ·············> 3 RAINBOW

"We made it past the Cave," says Dora. "So now we must go to the Troll Bridge."

Chapter 3
The Grumpy Old Troll's Riddles

When they arrive at his bridge, the Grumpy Old Troll tells them that they must answer his riddles.

"Here's my first riddle," says the Grumpy Old Troll. "He looks like a pony. On his head is a horn. What is he?"

Dora knows the answer to this riddle. Do you know the answer too? Yes! The answer is a unicorn, just like Unicornio! *¡Fantástico!*

But the Grumpy Old Troll has another riddle. "What grows from a seed when the rain showers? It can smell really sweet. What is it?"

Isa knows the answer to this riddle. Do you know the answer too? Yes! The answer is a flower. You are great at answering riddles.

Dora, Isa, and Unicornio can cross the Troll Bridge! Before they cross, though, the Grumpy Old Troll shyly asks one more question. "Isa, do you have any purple flowers? They're my favorite."

"I don't have any purple flowers, but I do have some purple flower seeds," answers Isa.

Isa plants the purple flower seeds. What do we say to make the flowers grow? *¡Crezcan, flores!* Say "*¡Crezcan, flores!*" Wow! The purple flowers are growing!

"Thank you," says the Grumpy Old Troll.
"I love purple flowers."

Chapter 4
The Giant Beanstalk

"We made it past the Dragon's Cave," says Dora, "and over the Troll Bridge. Now we go to the Rainbow. We're almost there!"

Do you see the Rainbow? Yes, the Rainbow is just behind Dora, Isa, and Unicornio. They hurry over to the Rainbow so Unicornio can go home and give the flowers to his *mami*.

But when they get there, the Rainbow is high up in the air.

"How are we going to get up there?" asks Unicornio.

Isa has an idea. "I have some beanstalk flower seeds that can help us."

Help Isa find the beanstalk flower seeds. Do you see them? There they are, in the bag with the green beanstalk on it.

Isa plants the seeds, but the seeds need to grow into a beanstalk before Dora, Isa, and Unicornio can climb up to the Rainbow. What do you say to make flowers grow? Say "*¡Crezcan, flores!*" The seeds are growing! Say "*¡Crezcan, flores!*" again. The beanstalks need to grow really tall. One more time. *¡Crezcan, flores!*

Great job! Now the three friends can climb up to the Rainbow.

"I can see the Unicorn Forest from here," cries Unicornio as they reach the Rainbow. "Let's go!"

Unicornio gallops across the Rainbow carrying Dora and Isa. "I'm home! I'm home!" he cries as the three friends enter the Unicorn Forest. He gives the unicorn flowers to his *mami*.

"My favorite!" says Unicornio's *mami*. "*¡Qué lindas!* How pretty!"

What a magical adventure! Thank you so much for coming along with Dora and Isa today as they helped their new friend Unicornio find his way home.

Dora's Great Big World

Dora

Dora loves to go exploring, especially with her friends and family. Continue reading to learn all about Dora's *amigos y familia*!

Boots

Boots is Dora's best friend. He always goes with her on her adventures!

Backpack

Dora carries Backpack with her wherever she goes. If Dora needs something on an adventure, Backpack is sure to have it!

Map

Who does Dora ask for help if she doesn't know which way to go? Map! Map always knows the way!

Isa

Isa lives in the Flowery Garden. She loves to grow flowers . . . almost as much as she loves helping Dora and Boots!

Unicornio

Unicornio is a friendly
unicorn who lives at the
end of the rainbow in an
enchanted forest.

The Big Red Chicken

The Big Red Chicken is very big
and very silly. He loves throwing
parties and doing magic tricks!

The Grumpy Old Troll

Before you can cross the
Grumpy Old Troll's bridge,
you have to solve his riddles!

Mei

Mei is Dora's
friend from China.

Najim

Najim is Dora's friend
from Egypt.

Mrs. FREUD

Mrs. FREUD

a novel

Nicolle Rosen

ARCADE PUBLISHING
NEW YORK

FIRST ENGLISH-LANGUAGE EDITION

First published in 2004 in France as *Martha F.* by Editions Jean-Claude Lattès

This is a work of fiction. Names, places, characters, and incidents are either the
products of the author's imagination or are used fictitiously.

Library of Congress Cataloging-in-Publication Data

    Kress-Rosen, Nicolle.
    [Martha F. English]
        Mrs. Freud : a novel / by Nicolle Rosen.— 1st English-language ed.
        p. cm.
    ISBN 1-55970-783-6
    1. Freud, Martha, 1861–1951—Fiction. I. Title.

    PQ2671.R445M3713 2005
    843'.92—dc22   2005010306

Published in the United States by Arcade Publishing, Inc., New York
Distributed by Time Warner Book Group

Visit our Web site at www.arcadepub.com

10 9 8 7 6 5 4 3 2 1

Designed by API

EB

PRINTED IN THE UNITED STATES OF AMERICA

Mrs. FREUD

1

Maresfield Gardens
September 23, 1946

Dear Mrs. Huntington-Smith,

Thank you for your kind letter. Today, on the occasion of the seventh anniversary of my husband's death, I received many expressions of sympathy, but of them all your letter touched me the most.

How could you think I had forgotten you? Your soothing presence seven years ago, at that most difficult and painful moment of my life, stands out in my memory as one of great comfort. After the terrible war years, when I felt especially isolated, I must tell you that receiving news from your distant America is a source of great pleasure.

I am afraid, however, that I must disappoint you, as I have to respond negatively to your request.

About writing my biography—overcoming my initial surprise, I fully appreciate that it is my life that seems to interest you and not that of my husband—all I can say is: How could I write about my life without mentioning him? You must understand that discretion and respect for the professor's privacy binds our family. My husband had always steadfastly discouraged anyone wishing to write his biography. Therefore, I cannot betray him.

The other reason for my refusing to cooperate with you is that, quite frankly, you, or any biographer for that matter, would have to characterize my life as essentially insignificant. Probing a little would quickly convince you, I am certain, that as a subject I do not offer much. I was fortunate to have married a genius, and during fifty-three years our marriage unfolded without the slightest cloud. Sigmund was the best of husbands, and as for me, I performed the role that was expected of me: a faithful partner whose mission was to organize a life sufficiently comfortable to enable my husband to construct his monumental oeuvre.

Reading between your lines, do I perceive that this project—were it to come to fruition—might serve the feminist cause? I frankly don't see how, and must dissuade you at once. You must understand that being a wife and mother was all I ever wanted. Both roles satisfied me fully. Rather dull and thin as a statement, don't you agree? My one-dimensional story could only remotely satisfy those readers with a penchant for indiscretion—you being excluded, of course.

Despite the disappointment my response will doubtless elicit, and for which I again apologize, may I kindly ask that you refrain from calling on other members of my family, especially Anna: you risk being badly received by her. She remains particularly sensitive to anything regarding her father.

Still, I can't help but be flattered by your interest, Mrs. Huntington-Smith, and look forward to hearing from you soon.

Warmly,

Martha Freud

P.S. Excuse my writing in German. Despite my long exile here, my English is still quite hesitant, and I have remained attached to Gothic writing.

2

When I saw the American stamp on the envelope, I assumed at first glance that the letter was from Oliver, or my sister-in-law Anna. What a surprise to see Mrs. Huntington-Smith's name! It had been so long ago. All of a sudden, things came flooding back. Sigmund's funeral. And the unexpected impression she had left with me that September 26, 1939, seven years ago.

War had started three weeks before. Everyone was living under some terrifying and obscure threat, and I was in deep shock from what had just happened. Sigmund had been so ill for so long; he had suffered horribly. The illness had distorted his emaciated face, his mouth was ravaged, it was truly horrific! It got to the point when I could no longer stand looking at him. And the smell . . . it was even keeping his dog away from him!

His last weeks had been dreadful for him and, needless to say, trying for me and all those around him. Death came as a merciful relief. What I didn't anticipate, of course, at the time, because I had lived for such a long time with sorrow, was the incredible void his death would create. Despair soon took over, opening the ground from under me, enveloping me in a black hole.

September 26, 1939

Golders Green, a charming place to which I often return. Its old stone benches, its ponds, its planters and arcades, remind me each time why I appreciate the English and their obsession with their gardens. It was a mild day, like today. Now and then the sun peeked out from between the clouds, warming the park's foliage still in its fullness, but there was already a hint of fall in the air. Eulogy succeeded eulogy, all laudatory and emotionally charged. Packed with personalities and celebrities, the impressive spectacle, which had been announced in the press, had also brought many curious onlookers, who had assembled outside. We had just returned from having witnessed the coffin's disappearance into the furnace. Overwhelmed with emotion, at that moment all I wished for was to breathe in the damp earth, the moist leaves.

Cremation has always troubled—even shocked—me. It goes against my deepest religious principles, despite the fact that I had renounced all religion during my fifty-plus years of marriage. But cremation had been Sigi's strict wish, I reminded myself. In keeping with his atheist beliefs, cremation would be passed on to the entire family, I knew. Except for my sister Minna, who had never turned her back on her religion and insisted we abide by all the rituals when her time came. As for me, I am not sure I will have the same courage. In any case, my spot has long been assigned and reserved in Sigi's urn. My ashes—what a lovely image—are to mix with his for all eternity.

That urn, an antique, had been a gift from Princess Bonaparte. I never really appreciated these old objects crowding our house, each requiring infinite patience and time to clean. This one was particularly distasteful to me, connoting inappropriate affectation for such a grave moment. Also, its pagan origin no doubt contributed to my displeasure. I had wished that Sigmund, despite his philosophical position, would find a way of affirming some kind of Jewishness during his life—and a legacy of some faith, however faint. I know, only classic antiquity interested him. No one around him ever discouraged that interest. But to come back to the urn, I can't help but think that it represented one more reason for me to harbor dark thoughts vis-à-vis this woman. How could I feel this about someone who had always shown us such generosity? Didn't we owe her our life? We did indeed! However, her putting herself forward a bit too much and too often is what irked me. I must also add that her attitude of *owning* Sigmund—I was of course aware of her actual financial investment in him—only added to my irritation.

Emerging from the crematorium, I was overwhelmed by an urge to be alone with my thoughts. I missed my sister, who was sick that day—her heart condition had worsened at the same time as Sigmund's health had declined—and now she could no longer leave her bed. Her absence today was all the more odd, an irony of fate, considering how close to him she had been for so many years. Like a sister, and no doubt more.

Pressing against me, people were offering condolences, close friends, less close ones, strangers. It was more than I could endure. I needed to sit on a bench and catch my breath. Surrounding me, my children were keeping an eagle eye on me. Especially Mathilde, who, I sensed, was particularly on the alert, ready to jump in at the slightest sign of my losing control. All of which should have been of comfort to me. Instead, an immense sense of solitude had taken hold of me, the profound notion that my life had irrevocably been emptied of all meaning.

Designated Sigmund Freud's official heir by her father, Anna was standing a few feet away, the center of attention, accepting all the homage.

I have no idea why, but suddenly I happened to notice in the crowd a young woman I had never seen before. I first took her to be one of Anna's assistants, but quickly realized she was much too elegant for that. In contrast with the princess, however, who was wearing an inappropriately ostentatious fur coat that day—and who by her name and fortune always managed to bring attention to herself—this woman's elegance was understated. A style altogether unknown to Anna, who long ago had started wearing a kind of uniform made of formless, ankle-length dresses—sacks she often sewed herself. Wearing her beret pushed low over her forehead, Anna had once and for all renounced all femininity, or any remote possibilities of seduction. She paraded as a spinster. Why had I not given her more of a sense of fashion? Thinking back, I realized that any advice from me, whether about her wardrobe or anything else for that matter, had never been welcome. . . .

It was clear that that young woman was not part of those courting Anna. In fact, she seemed to know hardly anyone except Dr. Jones, and was staring at me. After a short while, she walked over to me. I prepared myself for more solicitude, more praise of my husband.

"It's quite an ordeal, isn't it?" she said to me.

I assumed she was referring to the death of my husband.

"How difficult it must be to feel so utterly alone," she went on, "and know you virtually don't exist in the eyes of others."

Stunned, I remember staring back at her in disbelief. How could someone totally unknown to me utter such things? It seemed rude, indiscreet, borderline indecent. . . . My immediate impulse was to lash out. I didn't, of course. Something painful inside, something completely different from grief, was gnawing at me. Feeling no animosity, or even compassion, coming from her, I opted not to respond.

She sat down next to me and began speaking—without mentioning my husband's name, or the immense loss for humanity his death entailed; nor was she intimating any personal grief, for that matter. It was a relief to me. And, most unexpectedly, she began talking about herself. Born a Boston Brahmin, she was raised by nannies and sent to boarding schools, far from parents whose priorities were social obligations and charities. At eighteen, she had been pushed into a loveless marriage with an older man of her class. Predictably, the marriage collapsed, leaving her more alone than ever. An attempted suicide led her to one of my husband's pupils, Dr. Helene Deutch. Dr. Deutch managed to cure her and restore some meaning to her life. She divorced and moved to England, where she was working as a journalist and writer. In the context of an article she was writing about psychoanalysis in England, she had interviewed Anna and had hoped to do the same with my husband. But his illness had made that interview impossible. Now, to my utter bewilderment, she was expressing a desire to get to know me. Why? I kept wondering. I was listening the way a child listens to a scary story, the kind that sends shivers up your spine. She stopped speaking and handed me a card. She would contact me later, she said, and disappeared into the crowd.

I remained shaken all day, in a state of mind I couldn't fathom. No one seemed to notice, everyone being pre-occupied that day by so many other things. It wasn't only Sigmund's death that had thrown me into that state of mind, I realized. That American woman with her attitude and request to get to know me had rattled me.

Time passed, however, and I forgot all about Mary Huntington-Smith—until the arrival of this letter. Reading it awakened the same strange feeling in me as she herself had seven years before. Why, on this anniversary, where once again everyone had assembled to evoke the memory of the illustrious man, would a perfect stranger want to know about me, claiming it was of some interest to the rest of the world? Especially women.

I didn't hesitate. Refusing came easy to me. As always, I simply followed what seemed the proper course. Once again, I would act along the lines expected of me—displaying decency and discretion.

Her letter, however, had an unexpected and lingering effect I couldn't quite grasp. What was happening to me? This unknown woman meant nothing to me. She was neither a member of my family nor a friend, nor even someone recommended to me. Her request to know more about me was absurd and impossible. Also, hadn't my entire life been lived following clear parameters, never deviating from the rules? It had simply never occurred to me even to contemplate doing what was proscribed. The rules imposed by my milieu and family were absolute, and had molded my universe. I never felt any sense of sacrifice or regret. Why did this letter both intrigue and trouble me?

When, however, she clearly stated that the great man's life was not what she was after, I felt some kind of relief, even gratitude. No hint of disguised inquiry for a biography of Freud could be detected. Of course, I am well aware of the world's curiosity about famous men's lives and am under no illusion that, sooner or later, there will be many biographies of my husband—whether I like it or not. No, she had made her intentions eminently and unambiguously clear. Still, I had trouble accepting that it was *me* she actually wanted to know. Martha—the child, the young girl, the woman. The more I thought about it, the more it struck me as an unrealistic project. Nonetheless, her request made me realize that I had never opened up to anyone, starting with myself.

During the four years of our engagement, Sigmund and I wrote each other hundreds of letters. Reading this correspondence today, I see that my letters reveal nothing of any depth, or anything resembling the truth. I knew nothing about life—or myself. And how could I, with the education I received? It's clear that my goal had been to present to Sigi the image of the woman I knew he wanted—and such was my mandate for the next several decades. I so wanted him to love me! Endlessly anticipating his every wish was all I lived for. And mightn't that just be what love is all about? I must confess to being only half convinced by these lines. Aren't they perfect excuses for all the compromises, the little betrayals, I surrendered to during our life together?

I must also add that Mary's insistent request to know me triggered for the first time a private desire to look at my life, with all it entailed—despite my innate discretion. But I couldn't share this with an outsider. By immediately sending my refusal to Mary, I made certain not to succumb to that temptation.

Since that fatal September day in 1939 so much had happened, a mountain of painful events. Apart from the losses of so many around me, an increasing fear of the impending war permeated our lives. What would happen to the country where I was born? And to England, my second home? I must say, the bombings had little effect on me. I no longer bothered going down into the shelter. Having reached my advanced age, and suffered the deaths of so many I had loved, why should I care whether I died? All meaning had vanished from my existence so long ago.

Since the time of Mary's request, and not without trepidation—or even a modicum of guilt—I silently began the process of compiling the inventory of my life.

That my life had been entirely dictated by, and structured around, my husband's every wish was making it tricky to extricate the "me" out of it. It all seemed so preordained, so simple really. My actions, along with my thinking, had always been deeply connected and interwoven with Sigmund's—to the point where I was convinced some of the thoughts were my own. I couldn't help but wonder where the real "me"—if indeed there was a real "me"—had been hiding all those years. In the void that followed Sigmund's death, and from my new vantage point, I was—this was so new for me—questioning whether the good half-century of dedication, to the detriment of my own life and needs, was worth having been lived. Had I accomplished all I expected to? Was there nothing to regret? True, in the course of these past decades such questions had intermittently flashed through my mind, but they had quickly been banished. The time had come to revisit them.

Sitting in my room—our room—up on the second floor of my empty house, I stare at the two heavy beds that had followed us from Vienna. There they stood, as they always had, side by side. And for the past seven years I have been sleeping alongside an unopened, deserted bed. Probably longer, since Sigmund's last year was often spent working all night in his study under Anna's vigilant eye. Somehow, it hadn't occurred to me to get rid of the unused bed. I could have had it brought up to the attic or down to the basement. How would Anna or Mathilde—not to mention Paula, who had been with us since Vienna, and was now the keeper of the Freud Museum—have reacted to such a drastic move?

It was simpler to let it be.

Our first English abode on Elsworthy Road was far more modest. Sometime later, Ernst and Anna found this large, imposing redbrick house in Hampstead, nestled in a big garden. In charge of renovation, Ernst added a new veranda in the back of the house, and to spare his father and Anna from climbing the steep stairs leading to the bedrooms, he even had an elevator installed. The result was truly superb. We all enjoyed our new home enormously, especially the lovely garden, which seemed to us all a real luxury.

Back in Vienna, the only time we used to enjoy any fresh air was during our summer vacation, when each year we rented a house either in Grinzing, in the Wienerwald, less than two hours from the city, or up in the mountains. Our spacious new London house, with its own garden, simply enchanted Sigi. As for me, sitting, reading, or knitting under the big tree became one of my daily pleasures as well. During one of my garden reveries, I projected being there a long time, even welcoming the thought of one day falling permanently asleep under that lovely tree.

This said, twenty large rooms seemed a bit excessive for only five people. Especially compared to our Vienna life on Berggasse, where between our six children, Minna, and the domestics—not counting Sigmund's office—we had all fitted in nine rooms! It was tight, I remember, and there were plenty of times when we bumped into one another. I kept dreaming of leaving our apartment for a greener place, I recall.

Here in our new house, we had taken great pains to reproduce Sigmund's Vienna office. We knew how important it would be for him. We even managed to make his massive furniture, and all of Sigi's many small statuettes, find their equivalent Viennese spot in the new English surroundings. With its wide French doors opening onto the garden, Sigmund's lovely and majestic new office became his sanctuary—he simply loved the place. It is where he spent most of his time from then on.

Anna, responsible for everything regarding her father—a privileged responsibility he bestowed upon her—organized every detail and turned Sigmund's office into what has become, and is currently, the Freud Museum. Sigmund's original Viennese office, I understand, has also been turned into a museum.

I look out my window, perceiving the garden through a light English fog and drizzle. Getting accustomed to this climate, with its pernicious humidity, took some doing. I never stopped missing the stinging cold, the blankets of snow, the white roofs of Austria. To this day, I can't seem to ever get warm here. The wind seeps through all the windows of our modern house, and while our faces roast when we stand close to the chimney, our backs remain permanently frozen. Fighting this pervasive British damp is a losing battle. Images of our old Austrian furnaces made of ceramic tiles, from which a gentle heat emanated night and day, keep coming back. Not to mention our double windows with their thick drapes. I have never knitted as much as I have since I arrived in London: shawls, vests, scarves, and a number of sweaters. Minna knitted as well, as long as she was able to. Keeping warm seemed imperative to us. We had lost so much in the course of our lives: our country—the one I was born into and the one we lived in until we came to England—our language, our landmarks, our habits.

I must confess—without embarrassment, and despite all we have to be grateful for—my nostalgia for my native land. My childhood memories in Hamburg haunt me, my youth in Vienna, so much of my life spent in a place I considered mine, all of which left obvious deep marks. I was shaken upon hearing that the city I was born in had been obliterated. What about Wandsbeck, the small town where I spent my engagement years, which later became my mother's residence for the rest of her life?

I had to keep reminding myself that Austria and Germany—painful reality!—had become our enemies. Hating them for the horror, the massacre of millions of Jews—a fate from which we would not have escaped had we stayed—was nonetheless a new way of viewing what had once been my home, my country. I had trouble reconciling my memories with the terrible new reality. I can't help it, but German remains my native tongue, in which I read my favorite authors: Goethe, Schiller, Heine, and so many others. Furthermore, my country's food remains my favorite.

I hear the rattle of china downstairs. Paula must be setting the table in the parlor room. It is teatime, and Mathilde often joins us for tea. Maybe Lucy, pretty Lux—one of Sigmund's favorite daughters-in-law—will pay us a visit as well. Knowing Paula, she must surely have baked some sweets. Despite food restrictions, she continues to be resourceful and clever when it comes to finding or inventing ingredients, and improvising some potluck confection. She is a genius at substituting what is missing, and makes it a point of honor to present us each afternoon with a different cake.

Anna won't be coming. The English climate has once again gotten to her. She is down with some viral infection. In any case, she wouldn't have been here in the afternoon. She usually works in the nursery she has opened for children of the war, and meets Dorothy later. Right now, Paula is over there, nursing her. When Anna recovers, she and Dorothy will go to Amber Cottage, their house in the south of England.

What will become of me in this enormous house? Minna is no longer here. It has been five years since she died. I was so accustomed to her presence—she had lived with and next to me practically our entire existence. I even miss our quarrels. And today, without Sigmund, without Minna, I am for the first time lost—and bored. Astonishing as it may seem, shortly after their respective deaths, boredom entered as a new uninvited guest in my life. No longer having any precise task to perform left me startled, at a loss. After spending every minute for decades with a meticulously focused purpose, I was unprepared for this new unstructured life. Apart from the children's routine each day, I had learned to anticipate the precise moment when Sigmund would emerge from his office—and be ready for whatever he needed. Carefully overseeing his clothes every day—a detail near and dear to him—took a large place in my schedule. Then there were the holidays, each with its special set of meticulous preparations. Later, after all the children had moved out of the house, our own routine continued in the same strict way, my duties principally tied to Sigmund's needs.

With both Sigmund and Minna—my closest friend and most intimate enemy—gone, all I have left are the depressing needs of the old woman I have become. The terrifying void overwhelms me, and often I find myself bursting into tears for no apparent reason. Reading is no help. At my age, sleep is a problem. There are nights when I can't close my eyes, and negative thoughts have a way of engulfing me. Each evening, I brace myself for the nocturnal journey ahead, with its storms, its periods of calm. Wonderful Lux, my perfect daughter-in-law, gave me for my birthday a huge puzzle consisting of three thousand tiny pieces representing an artist's studio peopled with seated women, angels, paintings of all sorts and subjects hanging on its walls. Its dominant color is green, and I am delighted by it. "Won't such minuscule pieces ruin her eyes?" worried Mathilde. "Not really a gift for an eighty-five-year-old woman!" She went on looking at her sister-in-law reproachfully. I strained to explain to them both that, on the contrary, when I was faced with my solitude and all its ghosts, the puzzle was of real help to me. I had trouble falling asleep. Two months ago I had a large table brought up on which to spread the pieces of the puzzle, and each evening, like a faithful friend, it welcomes the old insomniac. Focusing on shapes and color, worrying where the fragments go, keeps my mind from fretting and has proved therapeutic. In two months, however, all I have been able to accomplish is to complete the border. Could British boredom be of such magnitude to have triggered this perfect remedy? Be that as it may, entering my bedroom and seeing the pieces all spread out, with the huge gap in the middle, is instantly reassuring. Whatever anxiety looms, I know will be obliterated. The puzzle is for me what sleeping pills are for others.

Teatime! Teatime! I hear Paula calling. Smiling, I go down. Funny how she has become more British than the British.

3

Maresfield Gardens
October 7, 1946

Dear Mrs. Huntington-Smith,

I must admit I was both surprised and delighted by your letter, convinced I had discouraged you earlier. That you are not in the least interested in any commercial endeavor, or any scandal for the sake of the sensational, greatly reassures me. I take this at face value, and apologize for having falsely perceived your intentions. Your desire to know me better touches me all the more in that you assure me of having renounced any thought of publication. The mere pleasure of engaging in a correspondence with you enchants me, for it will greatly differ from the one I have with old friends or family members.

This said, I must reiterate my earlier fear of disappointing you. True, I lived in Vienna, at the precise time when events changed the world forever; still, my testimony might not shed much light about that period for you, I'm afraid. You must remember that seeing to my husband's needs and raising my children were my main focus. Outside events, even shattering ones, remained somehow in the background, incomprehensible and remote. How did it feel living in the shadow of a great man? you ask. And did it satisfy me fully? Needless to say, these questions resonate deeply within me, and I haven't been able to answer any of them. Keeping these questions to myself all these years has made all my efforts to probe difficult, sterile.

My entire family, and all those around me, would be shocked, even scandalized, at the thought of my putting into question their credo. Had I not been a fulfilled wife? My marriage a perfectly happy one? Wasn't being part, however peripherally, of that great and important invention—psychoanalysis—not fully rewarding anyway?

I do welcome at last the opportunity to try and open up, unencumbered by any social or personal restrictions.

The perfect stranger you are makes our dialogue infinitely easier for me.

Being American—"a WASP," to quote you—young, independent and active, adds to the attraction, enabling me to speak freely as I never have with anyone until now. So much had been repressed over so many years. But my self-liberation has begun. Unlocking all that will be made easy precisely because you are so different from me—so far from me, and yet I feel I can trust you implicitly. There is so much I wish to talk about. I take you at your word that you will not use my letters for publication. I hope it is justified, my trust based on the memory, that painful funeral day seven years ago, of you as you came over to me, addressing me in simple and direct language—in contrast to the platitudes and de rigueur condolences that have beset and overwhelmed me these past several years. That memory of our encounter lingered with me for a long time.

You describe the beauty of your Indian summer. How I wish I could share the sight of those miles of flaming forests, dotted with sparkling lakes. Nature has always attracted me, but my knowledge is limited to my country's meadows and mountains. Sigmund and I shared that, although we never seemed to have pushed our curiosity beyond our familiar landscapes. What Sigmund enjoyed particularly was spending time in Italy. As for me, I never traveled beyond the German and Austro-Hungarian border, except in 1938, when we immigrated to England. Now my advanced age prohibits me from traveling outside Hampstead.

What fun it would otherwise be to discover the marvels of your country with you. I shall look forward to hearing further details about it. Without wanting in any way to offend you, I must nevertheless tell you that my husband did not like your country. I would even venture to say that Sigmund had developed a veritable aversion to it. When in 1909 he toured America, giving conferences, he developed an immediate dislike for everything: the manners, the food, the people, their lust for money. Later on in the course of our life, I was tempted to bring up the subject of immigrating to America, but immediately refrained, knowing full well that that was simply never an option for Sigmund.

How did the September 23 memorial go? you ask. It differed little from the actual funeral you attended, with the exception that there were fewer people. It was strict family and close friends this time. I used to appreciate gatherings of relatives at such anniversaries. In the course of years, as everything became darker around us, we reduced both its importance as well as the number of attendants. Strangely, and I don't know why, this anniversary was particularly painful. Did it underscore the terrible loss of the one to whom I had dedicated my whole life? I can't say. That's not all, I know. At Sigmund's funeral, you were the only one who showed great sensitivity, noting how alone I must have felt. I guess each of these memorials points up that same sense of solitude.

You were the only one at the funeral, I remember, to perceive the degree of abandonment I felt. Is it possible that those anniversaries trigger in me an echo of that abandonment? That day, two weeks ago, an overwhelming sense of artificiality took hold of me. Playing the role of widow—of a very old woman sitting in a chair, proffering banalities in response to the words of sympathy offered—also irked me. Like the small Viennese statuettes around me, the pictures of Sigmund on the walls, I too felt part of the inanimate scenery. The real focus, in all its dynamics, was being played outside me. My children and grandchildren were the actors, with Anna in the principal role. Dr. Jones came over and chatted with me. As you may remember, he is a charming and well-mannered gentleman. Having known him for over forty years, I have come to anticipate what he is going to say to me:

"How are you, Mrs. Freud?" Since all is well with my health, we quickly move on to the next subject, namely, my family. "What a splendid family you have, you must be so proud!" An obvious remark when it concerns Anna. Ernst too is remarkable. Not to mention young Lucien, who has already made a name for himself in the world of art! Not all my children are "splendid," but of course that concerns only me. Quickly gliding to the next topic, Jones continues: "What an extraordinary couple you and Sigmund made! Fifty years of marriage!" I correct him: "Fifty-three."

"Better yet! And without the slightest shadow! You have been the perfect spouse for an exceptional man! Without you, he simply could not have built his colossal work! Psychoanalysis owes you so much."

What he does in the course of his ritual speech is make sure he attracts the attention of the other people there, who on cue shake their heads, smiling approvingly. Once his little performance is over, he moves on, making a beeline toward Anna and proceeding to perform his second act of unsuccessful courtship. He is so amusing, that little man with his predictable manners and flatteries, his bald head, his piercing black eyes. With all his attempts, however, he has not yet succeeded in breaking Anna's resistance. She also knows full well, and resents, the fact that Jones favored her rival Melanie Klein, helping her settle and start her practice in England in 1926. I am sure you are familiar with such situations. Here, each child psychoanalyst claims to hold the key to her profession. No doubt the most important and influential person in British psychoanalysis today, Jones, an accomplished diplomat, carries on with Anna as if nothing had ever happened between them. It is all quite comical, really. All the more comical as the image of Jones in 1914 courting Anna, freshly arrived in England, comes flashing back. Jones was not yet married and had recently come out of a stormy relationship with one of Sigmund's patients, Loe Kann, when he turned his gaze on the boss's daughter. I'll never forget Sigi's rage at the thought of his daughter succumbing to this seducer! Promptly ordering Jones to cease and desist, he issued similar strict orders to Anna. "Jones would make a terrible husband," he insisted. Anna remained single, and Jones married twice. Today, both act as if nothing had ever happened between them.

Prevented by some princely obligation, and to Paula's great disappointment, the princess did not attend. Paula has an unhealthy fascination with the princess. Like many aristocrats, she addresses herself to the domestics of others as equals. Fully aware of how much Paula meant to Sigmund, Princess Bonaparte has done her level best to bring her close. I just received her letter with her royal husband's emblem, modestly signed "Marie Bonaparte." It irritated me. While she pretends to be like every other psychoanalyst, she clings to all the privileges her class and money dictate. As you have probably gathered, I never really cared much for her. As for Sigmund, he could not help being seduced by her adoration of him. He may even have been dazzled by a patient of such standing. Unfortunately, Sigi wasn't able to establish proper boundaries between the couch and family life. As a result, the princess quickly insinuated herself as a close friend, an indispensable ally. This said, I am aware that she is the one who helped us the most when we left Vienna. I can still see her sitting—camping, rather—on the stairs outside our apartment, with her pearls and mink coat, ready to block the Gestapo from entering. While I can never forget that she used everything in her power to save us—her title, her connections, her money—I still don't understand what the family sees in her.

Then there were all these women surrounding Anna. Strange, isn't it? Since at age twenty-five she decided to stay home and take care of her father, all Anna's charm had disappeared; she had lost all her femininity, and the spinster look took over. Her collaborators followed suit, dressing and emulating her look. She bossed them around, speaking in the voice of her father with religious authority.

The closest one to Anna is Dorothy Burlingham. How can I describe this tender friend, a tall American woman without much grace who, for the past twenty years, hasn't left

Anna's side? Here is a perfect example of my husband's mix of genders that Anna has adopted. Fleeing a husband who had—literally—lost his mind, Dorothy arrived in Vienna with her four children, whom she quickly placed under Anna's psychoanalytic eye while she was being treated by Theodor Reik. This was a godsend. Dorothy was a Tiffany, the American millionaire's daughter. Fees were paid in dollars, which in those difficult years was much appreciated. The two became inseparable, and Dorothy rented the apartment above ours, installing a phone between the apartments. Before we knew it, Dorothy was taking her turn on the master's couch. When summer vacation came around, Dorothy followed, renting near us, and in 1930 she bought her own house, where from that point on she, Anna, and the Burlingham children spent their holidays.

I always wondered how Sigi could have allowed himself to psychoanalyze a woman whose children were being treated by his daughter. All that while the entire group practically lived together. Was this perhaps his way to keep Anna close to him in yet one more respect? In his later years, Sigmund had taken to surrounding himself with worshipful women. In fact, the more rivalry among them, the better. Practically all Sigi's close male friends, those he had known since the beginning, had gone: Karl Abraham had died, Sandor Ferenczi and Otto Rank had distanced themselves from him. Women. Women. As is the case today, women constituted the ongoing court.

To come back to that anniversary afternoon: memories, anecdotes, were flooding my head. "This extraordinary man, that genius . . ." As more eulogies were dispensed ad infinitum, I turned to look at my middle-aged children, as if seeing them for the first time. There they all were, fully grown, with their salt-and-pepper hair, each with their respective baggage. Could I still call them my children? In 1918, I was the age Martin is today—fifty-seven. War had transformed everything, and I had trouble getting accustomed to the changes. Virtually oblivious to what was happening in the world then, I continued in my daily life to gravitate around Sigmund's every need, while he was increasingly focused on his career, his writing, and his patients. Today, after World War II—a war that far surpassed the first one in horror—everything is turned upside down, and this time it is too late for me to adapt to the changes. For my children, as for most younger people, life does go on, their profession, their love life, continuing to be the center of their preoccupations. Unable to catch up with their ongoing evolution, I feel increasingly left behind and estranged.

You interviewed Anna, I recall, and therefore probably know her a little. What about the others? They were six. I shall start with our eldest, Mathilde. With five younger siblings, all rather close in age, she managed poorly. As a young child, she was difficult, often sick—her way, I guess, of attracting attention. I only understood much later how she must have suffered. Irritated by her, Sigmund never grew close to her. Still, she grew into a shy, lovely young lady, and became much more calm and anxious to please. I remember how worried she was at not finding a husband, convinced she was unattractive. Her father had entertained the hope she would marry his Hungarian disciple Ferenczi—one of his favorites—but she ended up with Robert Hollitsher, a young man involved in some kind of business. The marriage turned out to be happy. Ferenczi was terribly attached to Sigmund, and that union would have been a disaster, considering how dependent Mathilde was on her father. As for Ferenczi's career, what would have happened had he become Freud's son-in-law?

Deeply unhappy at not being able to have children—a botched appendicitis operation early on had made her sterile—Mathilde managed nonetheless to go on about her life positively and actively. During the Depression, as her husband's business languished, she immediately opened a fashion shop, something she continued here in London. She is a sensible and solid person, and I always enjoy her company.

As for Martin, my second child, the first of my three sons, bizarre as it may appear to you, I find it hard to speak about him with objectivity. I don't really appreciate a lot of what he does. To give you but one example: at the recent memorial he showed up with an inappropriate exuberance. Everything concerning his father, including his memorial, turns into some excitement or juvenile celebration. That day, he circulated among the women, flirting with them indiscriminately—young, pretty, old, and ugly—going from group to group, chiming in with the chorus of anecdotes about his father and adding plenty of his own. Martin had a consuming passion for his father, a veritable cult attitude. Of all our children, Martin is the only one who moved right next to us in Vienna, on Franz-Josefkai, each day looking for some sign, some piece of advice, from his father. His law degree afforded him a position as attorney for the Psychoanalytical Society, another sure link to his father. What distinguished Martin was his athletic prowess and his way with women—neither of which I found particularly interesting. During the war the poor fellow was interned as a "foreign enemy" in Liverpool, a stigma from which he never recovered.

Even when he was young, I was less attracted to him than to the others. Who knows, his fixation on Sigmund might have been one of the reasons I kept my distance. Be that as it may, his general flightiness always irritated me. He and his wife Esti are separated; after a few years in France, she now lives in America with their daughter, Sophie. And their son, Anton Walter, left for Australia in 1938.

Martin was entirely responsible for the breakup of the marriage. He even had the gall to have an affair with one of Sigmund's patients, Dr. Edith Jackson—an unforgivable indiscretion. Whatever possessed him? Especially as he knew full well the degree of his father's sense of morality. In the end, his wife couldn't tolerate his infidelities. Curiously, Sigi did not agree with me, claiming it was Esti's independence that had been the cause for their separation—she was working as a speech therapist in those days.

I wonder whether, in openly having an affair with Sigi's patient, Martin wasn't trying to demonstrate something his father might possibly have dreamed of but never dared engage in. A bit twisted on my part, no?

As for Ernst, my fourth child, our third son, it is a whole different story. He was the only one to successfully detach himself from his father. In 1919 Ernst left Vienna for Munich and Berlin and, much against Sigmund's wishes, went on to study architecture. The houses Ernst ended up building were extremely modern, very much in keeping with the Bauhaus teachings and, needless to say, not to our taste. Sigi had remained quite conservative, and it didn't occur to me to think otherwise. Ernst married Lucy in Berlin. We named her Lux, the beautiful Lux. With her little turned-up nose, her upper lip slightly curled, she had Sigmund completely under her spell. It seems as though everything Ernst touched became instantly successful. His three sons, Stefan Gabriel, Lucien Michael, and Klemens Raphael—the three archangels, as we had named them—were all remarkable, physically and intellectually, and successful in their respective careers. I like to think that Ernst has inherited his father's talent without being stifled by him. Phlegmatic, well-mannered, impenetrable, and with a dry sense of humor that often startled me, he had lived in London since 1933, and could easily have been taken for a typical Englishman. At the memorial, he seemed slightly bored by the whole thing, as was I. The truth is, I have come to feel rather exasperated with the Freud cult. Since his death, Sigmund has become a saintly figure in the eyes of his followers, his life told and retold as a golden legend.

How Sigi would have detested all this! Or would he have?

To come back to Anna, our youngest—before I go on about her, how did you find her? Please rest assured that nothing you might say about her could hurt me. As you can see, I have been using a tone in no way resembling conventional discourse. I intend to keep nothing from you, and trust you'll do the same.

When I talk about my children, you'll note that the number does not add up to six. Two are missing: Oliver and Sophie. I never cease thinking about those two, whom I may even have considered my favorites.

With his big brown eyes, his dark locks framing an olive complexion, Oliver was often taken for an Italian child. My second son, our third child, I always found him touching as he labored with concentration over sophisticated construction games. He was sound of mind, coordinated, and neat.

Martin monopolized his father's attention, leaving little space for others, so getting close to his father was difficut for Oliver.

Oliver was mesmerized and dominated by his father. And like Martin, Oliver ended up without any significant career. In an effort to disengage himself from his father, Oliver emigrated first to France in 1933, and subsequently to America, where he still lives with his wife, Henny. I hope he has a good life there. Always concerned for Oliver, Sigmund mentioned obsessional neuroses, anal masochism, whenever he referred to him. Is it my doing? Did I show too much how I felt about him?

Then there is Sophie, who in 1929 disappeared forever at the age of twenty-six, leaving a destroyed husband, a six-year-old, and a thirteen-month-old baby.

"Our Sunday child," as we had called her, Sophie was tender and beautiful, someone who created harmony wherever she went. Those two favorite children happen to have been especially handsome. Since I always considered myself unattractive, could I have been drawn to these two especially because of their beauty? Sophie died within days of being struck down by the terrible influenza epidemic that was ravaging cities already decimated from the war. Due to some strike, no trains were leaving Vienna, and traveling to Hamburg was impossible. We never made it to her bedside in time.

We were inconsolable. Minna had just emerged from a serious pleurisy, and I from a nasty pneumonia. Why had we, old ladies, been spared instead of this beautiful young mother? The question would remain forever unanswered. Of course, no one was to blame, Sigmund insisted. But how could this heal our broken hearts? Coping with our despair and our sorrow was all that was left for us.

What kind of mother have I been? I recently have been asking myself. Not the hugging or kissing type, certainly. In this respect, Sigmund was far more affectionate than I. He often delighted in taking the children on his lap, something I never did. When I was young, I thought of myself as a perfect mother, and in those days no one dissuaded me. A perfect wife, I was also called. But it no longer has any meaning for me. In those days, you must remember that when children were born, a nanny entered the picture. This applied to all six of my children. After the nanny came the maid, whose responsibility was to feed, wash, clothe, and even take on part of the children's education. I was brought up the same way. This said, I wasn't an absent mother. I oversaw everything concerning my children. As they grew, I took personal care of their education. I believe I was a good educator. Strict, yes, but nevertheless affectionate—or at least, as much as my nature permitted.

Like my mother before me, I became a woman whose only mission was performing perfectly all the domestic tasks required, without showing much emotion. If and when a child got hurt, I never panicked but directed the maid to call the doctor. Martin recalls how utterly calm I was when one day, after jumping up and down when he was little, he injured himself. Was I impervious to his pain? I was sitting near him, occupied in some manual work, and calmly waited for the maid to call the doctor. Other mothers would have undoubtedly behaved with more emotion. In any case, when Martin retells the story today, I still detect reproach in his voice.

Did my lack of tactile warmth affect my children, and if so, to what degree? Pondering this today, I realize that my nature, perhaps too rigid and repressed, was not the sole cause. It had more to do with the fact that the center of my life was really my husband, not my children. The situation was rendered even more complicated when my sister Minna came to live with us. It must have been clear to all that both of us planets gravitated around the sun that was Sigmund; both of us lived for his every gesture. How could my children not have been aware of it, and not suffered? It was unavoidable. Some of our children were sucked into the same vortex and, like Minna and I, were drawn to their father like moths to light. The ones who managed to move away not only escaped but protected themselves as well. In that respect, Ernst fared the best.

I can't remember at what moment the feeling of detachment from everything surrounding me took hold, or when I acknowledged my solitude. Was it after my husband died? No, it pre-dates that. Some twenty years ago I lost all reason to live. It happened subtly, without my noticing it. Motives? I wouldn't know where to begin. They are so numerous, so private. I would have to start from the beginning, from the early days of my marriage. Further back even, to the beginning of my life—an endeavor so overwhelming, I lack the strength to confront it.

It happened quite a while ago, even as far back as when I was first engaged, then as a young bride, and later as a young mother. Some claim it is a normal evolution in any relationship, especially one that lasted as long as ours did. But once I found myself out of that place, what was there left for me to do? The upkeep of the house no longer rested on my shoulders. Domestics were assuming that role quite efficiently without much interference from me. I merely went through the motions. From her arrival in 1929, Paula, that young and charming young lady, took over the basic housekeeping and quickly became fully in charge. As a girl freshly arrived in Vienna from the country, Paula could have married any middle-class man. But she was afraid of men and remained a virgin, attached to one master. Her devotion to our family was total. With her typically Austrian face, her bright blue eyes, her blond curls, she conquered my husband in no time at all. She also quickly understood the dynamics of our family hierarchy. First came the professor, who was to receive all her attention. The fact that he was famous was an added bonus, and she basked in the reflected glory. Sigmund soon became Paula's idol. Minna tried to lower her in Sigmund's eyes but quickly backed off, resigning herself to Paula's essential role in running the household. Surprisingly for Minna, she understood that avoiding any confrontation with this formidable young woman was a good idea. And besides, there was a whole other issue for Minna at the time—Anna's rising influence with Sigmund, which dethroned her a little more each day. Perceiving the change of guard, Paula knew right away how to deal with Anna. And today, when Anna has replaced her father as the eminent figure in psychoanalysis and is sitting at the top of our pyramid, Paula's devotion is directed only to her. She reports to Anna on all manner of things, from housekeeping to accounting. What about me?

you might ask. While it had been clear from the start that Paula respected me as the wife—she even accepted my role as head of housekeeping—make no mistake, I was never anything but second fiddle in her eyes. There were times I glimpsed and imagined pity emanating from her. Intolerable, perhaps, but I did nothing to correct it.

Today, with the passing years, Paula has become a precious friend, often the only one still with me in this large, empty house, and I frequently go downstairs for the sake of exchanging a few words with her. Anna is so busy, and gone most of the time. And frankly, we don't really have much to say to each other anyway.

Dear Mrs. Huntington-Smith, while what I write may have some meaning for me, it must surely be very boring to you. Do let me know what exactly you would like me to talk about. I'll try not to ramble too much. Does what I write about represent an interest for anybody?

Warmly,

Martha Freud

4

Why could I not bring myself to reveal to Mary that the person I most missed is my little sister Minna — a surprising revelation, to say the least, improbable and even incomprehensible? I am certain that those around me wondered how in the world I could have endured for forty years the presence of someone in my home who undeniably played the role of a rival. Looking back, I must say, it baffles even me.

It all goes back to when I was four years old, in Hamburg. I turned away from my mother as she proudly held a crying infant I found ugly. "This is your new little sister," she said. "Aren't you pleased?" I obviously wasn't. I found her horrible, in fact, but I knew enough to take her question as an order, and thereafter offered to help with the baby, pretending it pleased me.

This image, engraved in my memory, often recurred intact, symbolizing my feelings for Minna: I *had* to take care of her, while enduring her disagreeable presence. That nagging duality persisted throughout the inexplicable closeness of our long life together.

I would see my mother's approving looks as I assumed my role of good and affectionate older sister to what I really considered a repellent infant. And so it continued for many years. Minna's temperament didn't improve as she grew; in fact, she would kick and scream and roll on the floor at the slightest order — a sure way to always obtain what she wanted.

Needless to say, an acute sense of injustice was born in me then, and I increasingly resented the whole situation. Why was it Minna could get away with behaving like a brat, while I, docile and helpful, got not the slightest recognition? Often the fate of the oldest child, I know.

We were so different: I obedient and sweet, with a pathological tendency to remain constantly in the background; Minna often brutally outspoken, and always in some kind of confrontation or rebellion. My practical sense stood at the opposite pole from her need to be perceived as an intellectual. Despite her strictness and unfairness, I loved my mother. Minna hated her.

How, you might wonder, with all these differences, did we end up as adults living side by side under the same roof, for all those years? It did seem to both of us the natural thing to do at the time. Anyway, I never questioned it. In those days, families always rallied when a member was in need. But today I am trying to understand the chain of events that led to that situation. It was 1896. Sigmund and I had been married for nine years, and I had just given birth to Anna. I was exhausted by my endless pregnancies—this was my sixth, and it had been an especially difficult one. Minna, for her part, had lost her fiancé some eleven years before. Living alone, she had been taking jobs as companion to various ladies. A letter we had just received from her mentioned her hesitation in accepting yet another such job in Frankfurt. Tired of being a glorified domestic, and aware of my state of immense fatigue, she asked whether she could for a short while be of some help to me. Sigmund and I registered her letter as a clear SOS. "Why not?" said Sigmund. "You are tired. She'll be of assistance to you." So by return mail we invited her to come. She and I would resume our previous closeness, I convinced myself, and anyway, in my distressed physical state, I was looking forward to having a woman around. She could, and would, relieve me of some of the children chores.

We did share a strong family sense: helping one another in times of distress seemed the normal thing to do. Once she settled in our home, however, reality predictably unfolded in a much more complicated way. The details I am about to go into are rather unpleasant to me. I had been aware, at the time of our engagement, of a friendship between Sigmund and Minna, a friendship that was to evolve into a very strong and close relationship. Both shared the same turn of mind, an endless intellectual curiosity. This similarity, Sigmund made sure to tell me one day, was precisely what would have made marriage between them impossible, whereas I "possessed everything he lacked: patience, calm, and kindness." That argument, I recall, left me partially reassured. Why would he have mentioned marriage between himself and Minna? That it had even crossed his mind earlier as a possibility troubled me to no end. But as the years rolled on, I ended up not worrying about it anymore. Wasn't he treating Minna like a sister? — a sister he was very fond of, granted. I managed to convince myself. Anyway, at the time of my own engagement, Minna herself had gotten engaged to Ignaz Schonberg, a twenty-one-year-old student of Oriental philosophy, a friend of our brother's. He was perfect for her. She had found her intellectual match. I disliked him from the moment I met him. Only interested in himself, he adored listening to the sound of his voice. Furthermore, I found him ugly, with his scraggly, unbecoming beard. Not that Minna was particularly beautiful, for that matter. I reconciled myself by deciding they were made for each other.

Ignaz accepted a teaching job at Oxford and left two years later without telling anyone when he might return. That seemed odd to me, although at about the same time Sigi and I were engaged but separated as well. Felled by tuberculosis, Ignaz left Oxford, and instead of growing closer to Minna, he retired into his own family, broke off his engagement, claiming he was giving Minna her freedom back because of his illness. Sigmund and I knew that neither he nor I would have conducted ourselves like that, and concluded that had if he really had loved Minna, he would have behaved differently.

Minna was too intelligent not to see this. But when he died in 1885, she nonetheless assumed the role of widow—an easier role probably than admitting she had attached herself to a fool who had dropped her.

There was never to be any other beau in her life. (Her disagreeable personality didn't help.) Giving up all pretense, she carried on as a spinster from then on. When in 1896 she moved in with us, the only available room for her was the small one right next to ours. The problem was, for her to get to her room, she had to go through ours—a most embarrassing situation both for us and for her. Surprisingly, however, I seemed to have been the only one to object. And so life went on, with my sister blithely crossing our bedroom whenever she needed to. When, years later, the children had moved out of the house, Minna did take over one of their rooms. What was most astonishing to me, however, was that she never bothered to settle into a proper bedroom of her own, simply continuing to sleep in the same small place right next to us, without its own access.

She had come for "only a short while." She never left.

Before long, Minna occupied a larger and larger place in our home, and within ten years she became gigantic, gaining a good seventy pounds as she waddled her enormous self through our life. Even her voice had taken on surprising volume as it resonated between our walls. As for her self-importance, it grew with the rest. She succeeded in turning her tiny room into the center of our house. I was upset, but in my exhausted, low-energy post-birth condition, I somehow could not muster the strength to have any kind of say in the matter. Life went on, with Minna marching ahead of us all.

Sigmund, for his part, was delighted. He seemed to have adopted Minna as a kind of colleague, sharing all sorts of professional details with her, his face lighting up whenever she appeared in the room. Systematically excluded from their discussions regarding his research or work, I had been relegated to the role of outsider. I watched them as they talked animatedly to each other, sharing jokes at the dinner table, often repairing to a game of cards in the evening. Sigmund's manuscripts were given only to Minna for her approval and corrections. Needless to say, I was deeply hurt by this, but I nevertheless went on in my wifely role, coming to peace with the situation and concluding that Sigi needed both of us—I, in the role of Martha-the-mother-sweet-natured-one who directed the flow and comfort of his daily life, and Minna, the colleague and playmate in whom he could confide about all that preoccupied him, intellectually or otherwise. They traveled together, even frequently visited spas. Did that seem right to me? Ultimately, I must have been in a numbed state.

"No question, those two must be having an affair!" I knew was being whispered around. I chose to ignore what they were saying. While Minna's presence and increasing closeness to Sigmund was making me terribly unhappy, any amorous relationship between them was ruled out, in my mind. It seemed so absurd; Minna was so unattractive, completely devoid of charm with her bloated face, her deformed body. Why would Sigmund find anything in her other than a close friend? There were plenty of young, beautiful, available, adoring ladies around to tempt him. But his morality was irreproachable. He would never have committed adultery.

As I look back on all that, there is no doubt in my mind that Minna was in love with him, from day one. And Sigmund had to have known it but, never giving her any hope, went on enjoying her company—without ambiguity, as far as he was concerned. If in the course of their travels early on, temptation had raised its head, I know in my heart of hearts that Sigmund would never have succumbed. His commitment to me was absolute. True, he enjoyed the company of women, especially those who worshiped him, and there was always a nice supply of those around him. Coming from a home where he had been cherished by women—his mother and sisters—the company of intelligent ladies seemed natural to him.

Am I trying to convince myself, to fool myself? And how can I be so sure about what really went on, anyway? Is it possible that I wasn't jealous of Minna, being fully aware that during their frequent trips they stayed in the same inns? Yet in those days, for some strange reason, I had complete trust in them both. What did make me suffer, however, and greatly so, was their complicity, which radically excluded me, making me feel abandoned. The jealousy I felt then reminded me of how I had felt as a little girl, when it became clear to me that Minna had become my mother's favorite. While I bitterly resented the place Minna came to occupy in Sigi's life, Minna nevertheless through the years had become an important, and necessary, presence for me as well. As the gap between Sigmund and me became unbridgeable, I found myself depending increasingly on her company. It made me feel less alone, and through her reports I kept abreast of Sigmund's work and projects.

It is late, darkness has descended outside, I can no longer distinguish the end of the garden, the first streetlights have just been turned on, and I am suddenly quite tired.

5

Maresfield Gardens
October 22, 1946

Dear Friend,

Thank you for your prompt reply. I find myself anticipating and looking forward to your letters. And it reminds me of when Sigmund and I were engaged, and how important the mailman's visits became. Of course, mail came more frequently in those days, given that the distance between us was shorter.

You mention in your letter how unpleasant Anna had been to you in the course of your interview seven years ago, and that she pointed to your nationality as a deterrent. It does not surprise me. She has adopted, without any personal experience of her own, her father's dislike of America. I have to believe that her friendship with Dorothea can only be explained because Dorothea had turned her back on her country.

Also, she couldn't forgive you, I'm sure, for having interviewed Melanie Klein before you interviewed her. When it comes to being faithful to her father, Anna is unbending. In that, she is absolute. She simply cannot forgive anyone who strays from that dictum. That is what governs her every judgment—with everyone. She never forgave Eva Rosenfeld, her closest friend, for having chosen her rival to analyze her. None of Eva's subsequent efforts at contrition altered Anna's rigid position. My daughter's personality is extremely difficult.

Do I have a particular problem with Anna, you ask? The answer takes me far back, to well before she was born. As a young girl, my dream was that when I married, I would have three children, no more. I had no desire to emulate my mother, or Sigmund's, both of whom spent their lives focused on raising large families. After my fifth child, I realized that my husband, though a doctor, seemed to have no clue about how to avoid getting me pregnant. As a result, I found myself willy-nilly in my mother's and mother-in-law's exact life pattern, with all the predictable fatigue, wear and tear, and inevitable touch of depression. What undoubtedly contributed to my state of mind then was my married life. It had taken a decidedly different turn to the one I had dreamed about. From the very beginning, when I first met Sigmund, it was clear to me that his work represented the core of his life. But as time went on, it became increasingly worse: we spent hardly any time alone with each other. What was left between us were only the most mundane conversations relating to the quotidian. Long gone was the passion of our engagement. This change, now I think of it, took place abruptly, almost from one day to the next, right after our marriage. Even before our first child was born, affection had replaced passion. I consoled myself with the notion that passion was merely ephemeral: if in its wake it left something good, that was fine. What I most missed and longed for was not so much the passion but the wonderful rapport we had shared during our long engagement. In those days, we told each other everything. My first sense of being abandoned dates back to that moment, shortly after our marriage, which I have just mentioned.

The family I had produced soon occupied me fully, taking my all, and becoming a wall between Sigmund and me—in fact, between the world and me. For Sigmund's sake, daily routine needed to be played out without the slightest glitch. I did give it an honest try, having been groomed for the task. I had even gained the reputation of being a perfect housewife, which made Sigmund proud. In reality, however, my heavy agenda was often overwhelming, making me vulnerable to dark thoughts I kept to myself. You are the first, after my mother, in whom I have confided.

In the spring of 1895, I remember, something odd happened. I stopped menstruating and immediately assumed it was a sign of early menopause. I wasn't yet thirty-four. How could this be? Strange, but my doctor of a husband didn't disabuse me. Or, perhaps, could I have kept this from him? I don't recall. Be that as it may, what was happening of course was simply the start of my sixth pregnancy—and that devastated me. Barely able to make ends meet in those days, with Sigmund deep in research, we were besieged with domestic, financial, and parental problems. Our five children and Sigi's busy schedule seemed all we could embrace. We didn't yearn for more at the time. While Sigmund's physical desire had somewhat decreased in recent years both in intensity and regularity, he nonetheless was pursuing me—without ever taking preventive measures of any kind. Over the next nine months, I was deeply depressed. Had I ultimately turned into a baby machine like my mother? A quick calculation of my forthcoming fertile years made me look upon the future with a frisson.

Taking courage in my hands, for the first time—I recall being terribly embarrassed, for we had never broached this kind of subject together—I spoke with my husband and shared my anxieties with him. He listened attentively and, after a long pause, responded by saying there was only one solution to the problem. He didn't elaborate, but I soon found out for myself. Meanwhile, on December 3, a baby girl was born. Sigmund insisted on naming her Anna. For his older sister? He didn't really get along with her. No, it had to do with a relative of Dr. Hammerschlag's, who had taught him the Scriptures, he claimed. But the more Sigmund denied, the more I wondered whether I hadn't been right. Sigmund's very intense relationships with the women in his family, especially his mother, led me to his sister. As for the boys, they all had been given names of famous people: Charcot, Cromwell, and Professor Burke. This seems to go back to Sigmund's childhood. Already, as a ten-year-old, he had managed to impose on his parents the name Alexander—as in Alexander the Great—for his younger brother.

Unlike all my previous pregnancies, this one proved particularly difficult, and while I am loath to confess this, soon after the baby was born, I turned away from her. Was it exhaustion? The baby? General postpartum depression? I couldn't tell, and although a good mother would never do such a thing, I found myself unable to show any maternal feelings for that sixth baby of mine. Unlike the other children, Anna didn't have a wet nurse, and was given the bottle right away. We entrusted Anna—along with Ernst and Sophie—to Josephine, a new nanny who, as if sensing what Anna lacked, gave her the lion's share of affection.

Although Sigmund had been a very attentive father to all his children, it soon became clear that Anna had conquered her father's heart. I had thought that pretty little Sophie would have been the one, but early on, bright and spunky Anna became the apple of Sigmund's eye. Was he compensating for my lack of affection? Or was the undivided passion Anna had for him simply irresistible? Whatever the reasons, Anna held the place of choice with Sigmund. As for me, it was no more than a superficial relationship.

Unbeknownst to all, those years were extremely hard on me. I made certain to keep my discouragements, my doubts, and my concerns from Sigmund and appeared in charge and efficient, both as wife and mother. It would never have occurred to anyone that most of what I did was in fact leaving me terribly frustrated. With my increasingly famous husband and my six children, wasn't I a blessed woman? It would never have occurred to Sigmund that I was anything but happy and fulfilled.

I must ask to be forgiven for revealing such intimate details to you—I shall confess, and that only to you, that following Anna's birth, as a means of contraception, Sigmund decided unilaterally to practice chastity. I was thirty-five. How did I feel about it? Perplexed, to be sure. But what I missed most was the tenderness these moments generate. Nothing ever replaced that for me, and this must account for my depression, which reached its peak that summer.

In addition, the arrival of Minna into our home, under the pretext of helping me (but clearly to get closer to the brother-in-law she adored), only compounded the problem, I am certain. Things soon became unbearable. Without admitting it to myself, I was no doubt jealous. As I write, I am somewhat stunned, for I have never revealed any of this to anyone. And while I am in the confiding mode, I might as well reveal another source of that less than honorable feeling, jealousy, for which I am profoundly embarrassed. Someone else had entered Sigmund's life. Not a woman, no. Shortly after Mathilde's birth in 1887, Sigmund met Wilhelm Fliess, a laryngologist from Berlin. This eminent doctor had made a huge impression on Sigmund, and for the next fifteen years he became his close friend, confidant, and master, usurping my role once and for all. I could not have anticipated the intensity that such a male friendship would take on. Sigmund's relationship with Fliess took the place of all relationships, mobilizing all Sigmund's feelings. Sigi had literally fallen under Fliess's spell, a condition I had been familiar with, and of which I represented a prime example. A correspondence between them began, followed by regular visits. In Wilhelm, Sigmund had found not only a colleague and friend but a fellow combatant. Fliess, like himself, was deeply engaged in important medical research. In their respective disciplines, both were convinced they would change the world.

I, too, found Fliess attractive. He was married to a Viennese woman, and the four of us often went out together. In our outings, as I chatted with her, I could see from the corner of my eye how animated the two men were becoming as they conversed. Their eyes shone, their complexions became rosier, as they excitedly exchanged thoughts. They were sailing together on the high sea of medical discovery, leaving us behind, excluded.

Of the same height, similar corpulence, identical black beards framing their faces, the two men could have passed for brothers. Similar backgrounds of middle-class businesspeople, as well as being doctors and Jewish, made them a perfect fit.

Wilhelm, unlike Sigmund, however, had begun his professional life more auspiciously from the financial viewpoint. Twenty-one when his father died, he promptly began his medical practice after graduation, opened a clinic, and became immediately successful. I often found myself envying his wife, and their life, free as it was from all financial constraints.

Eleven years before, Sigmund had returned from Paris after working with Professor Charcot. Ever since, finding a definite cure for hysteria had been all that preoccupied him. The year was 1889. Sigmund, deeply immersed in his research, agitated and anxious, was totally dissatisfied with his efforts. But he no longer shared his concerns with me, only with Wilhelm.

When little Mathilde was twenty-two months old and I was pregnant with Martin, Sigmund left for Nancy, France. He worked on his hypnosis technique with an obscure private physician, Dr. Liebault, and his follower, Dr. Bernheim, and continued on to Paris to a congress, bringing along one of his patients to meet the two masters. It turned out to be a major fiasco. Sigi returned home deflated, convinced that his technique wasn't solving the illness's problems, and immersed himself more deeply in his research in the hope of improving his cure. That same year, he borrowed from his friend Dr. Breuer something called the cathartic method, which led him to apply his "technique of concentration." It consisted of asking the patient to focus on only one symptom and recall everything pertaining to that symptom. When one of his patients one day complained that Sigmund had interrupted her description too soon, it gave him pause. Thus was born the method that was to become psychoanalysis's number-one rule—free association.

As someone whose role was caring for the house and children, you will no doubt be astonished by my use of psychoanalytic jargon, which seems to come out of nowhere. You are the first and only person, Mary, to whom I have revealed this bit of knowledge, having been aware all along that stepping out of my prescribed role would worry everyone around me. Minna, and later Anna, were the only two family members privy to Sigmund's work, and both of them fiercely protected that privileged position. In all fairness, I must recognize that in those early days I knew practically nothing about Sigmund's professional preoccupation. His secrets were kept within the confines of his office. It is also true that, as a young bride, I was convinced that Sigmund was treating his patients as any normal doctor would coming out of medical school. That Sigmund was considered a giant among the makers of the modern mind, and was in fact turning medicine upside down forever, radically questioning everything, was unknown to me in those days. It was only after opening his books, secretly at first, then openly since his death, that I discovered his *Study of Hypnosis*, written with Joseph Breuer, in which I recognized the case of my friend Bertha Pappenheim, appearing under the name Anna O., which Sigmund had mentioned to me during our engagement years. Only then did I fully understand for the very first time what had preoccupied him so at the time.

Bertha was a very serious young lady, and my mother

liked her and encouraged our friendship. All of a sudden, one day, she became seriously ill. Her mysterious illness manifested itself in partial paralysis and, at times, an inability to swallow. Or—upsetting those around her and without any warning—she would suddenly break into English! I have since learned that this is called hysteria. I remember Sigi telling me then that she had gone to seek help from his friend Joseph Breuer. The treatment, alas, did not work. Breuer's wife, in whom he had confided his failure, encouraged her husband to stop the treatment. Hearing that decision, however, Bertha—who, it turned out, had a crush on her doctor—apparently went into a convulsion, claiming for all to hear that she was about to give birth to a baby—whose father was Breuer! All of which was pure nonsense, pure fabrication. Nonetheless Breuer panicked, opting as a measure of last resort to perform hypnosis on Bertha—following which he promptly left, taking his wife on a hastily prepared trip in the hope of obliterating any ambiguity or feeling of betrayal his wife might have harbored. His repair job worked. Nine months later, Breuer's little girl was born.

Meanwhile, Sigmund took all this very badly, I remember, condemning Breuer's behavior as an ethical breach, incensed that his friend had abandoned his patient. In my supreme ignorance and naïveté, upon hearing the story, I took Mrs. Breuer's side and applauded this denouement. Bertha, it turned out, got better, and is currently working in Germany with orphans who escaped from the Russian pogroms of 1881. Ever since that bizarre episode, I often worried that a similar thing could happen to Sigmund: despite his insistence, he was far less seductive than Breuer!

In those days I was unaware of Sigmund's audacious hypothesis that the origin of all neurosis is sexual. This is why, I later learned, that after 1885, Sigmund stopped working with Breuer. His friend's attitude in the case of Bertha convinced Sigmund that Breuer had not evolved in matters of sexuality. It surprised, even shocked, me to witness how Sigmund turned against his friend. How could this incident be the reason for ending such a long friendship? When Breuer refused to accept repayment of debts from Sigi (debts accrued during medical school, and at the time of Sigmund's setting up his office), this was the last stroke. Sigi flew into a violent rage against the man who had once been his close friend. This would not be the last time: several times in the course of our life I would witness similar behavior from him to colleagues, who became close friends and were later summarily dropped by Sigmund for one reason or other.

This rupture, I am certain, was not unrelated to Sigmund's deep and recent friendship with Wilhelm Fliess—an all-encompassing relationship that simply couldn't suffer any competition. This was 1896, and my husband was depressed. His book on hysteria had been poorly received; Vienna's medical establishment was snubbing him. How could they continue to take his work seriously? was their reaction. And besides, their message to him was loud and clear: the whole subject of hysteria lacked any interest whatsoever! Sigmund reacted immediately by affirming his position, declaring once and for all that sexuality was the origin of all neuroses, and proceeded to coin the term *psychoanalysis.* Hypnosis had definitely been replaced by free association.

In the meantime, what troubled me more was Sigi's increasingly tight relationship with Wilhelm, one that bordered on passion, it seemed. I do not say this lightly. The fact is, Sigmund would closet himself in his office for hours, writing endless letters to Fliess. He lived for their meetings, which he called *"congresses,"* and I saw with utter dismay how, when these had to be postponed, Sigmund would fall into deep despair.

All this left me terribly discouraged. What had happened? Had I lost my place in my husband's life? What had my role become? My daily domestic activities suddenly became empty of meaning, and for the first time I too lost my desire to go on. The dreams and hopes of my youth had now irrevocably been relegated to memory. I dreaded the road ahead that, I sensed, would from now on be tedious, long, and monotonous. The utopian happiness I had kept expecting to materialize had just evaporated.

All this seems so distant to me now. Everything was so different then. You didn't know that era, dear friend, you who were born in 1910. Those were the days of horse carriages, corsets, dresses with hoops, when men wore frock coats and top hats. The order that governed people's lives was a given, unshakable. Each in his place, each his or her prescribed role.

Jews were congregating in Vienna each year in larger numbers as they fled persecution elsewhere. Here they felt safe, especially compared to the dangers they found in other countries. Here in Austria, their kind, all-mighty emperor protected them. His authority guaranteed them rights as well as safety for all time to come. When Franz-Joseph took the throne in 1848, he instituted a new law under which Jews were entitled to the same status as all the other citizens of the Austro-Hungarian empire.

This said, anti-Semitism was on the rise in Austria, doubtless because of the influx of Jewish immigrants. Still, as long as it didn't express itself too aggressively, and wasn't considered official, Jews went peacefully about their lives, protected by the law. They could work as they pleased, live where they wished.

In our house, we had made it an unwritten rule to keep to ourselves, avoiding goyim as much as possible. When in 1869 my parents arrived in Vienna, we lived at 3 Rembrandtstrasse, in Leopoldstadt. This section of town, we had learned, had been named in honor of a seventeenth-century emperor who became famous for having chased Jews from the city. When my parents returned to Vienna, they settled in that part of town. Half the Jews in Vienna lived in Leopoldstadt, which was subdivided into smaller districts. Those near the Augarten or the Prater were the most elegant. The less fortunate lived in Brigittenau, or even farther out, in Ottakring or Hernals. As for us, part of the middle class and devoid of fortune, we lived in the middle section. The really rich, like the Rothschilds and Oppenheimers, occupied fancy apartments near the Ring. In 1869, construction of the beautiful avenue encircling the old city was completed.

If you have been to Vienna, you have no doubt seen that Leopoldstadt worked well for its purpose. This part of town and Brigittenau lie in a kind of narrow island. At the northeast end runs the Danube, with the Donaukanal at its southwest. To enter Leopoldstadt, you need to cross one of the bridges over the canal. I always assumed that the bridge at the end of our street was more like a border, dangerous to cross, than a mere passage. We lived among ourselves, exclusively with people of our own milieu and religion. The only non-Jews I knew in my childhood were our maids—blond girls with rosy cheeks who had come from the country to find jobs as domestics in the city.

What strange times! How could middle-class families without much fortune afford several maids? We never had fewer than two, and after my marriage there were five servants in our Bergstrasse apartment. Poorly remunerated, and sometimes not paid at all, they often slept in the most rudimentary conditions, even in corridors and kitchens, and were grateful to exchange the utter misery of their country life for even modest room and board. In those days, this was the norm. With little or no scruple, everyone went along with this. We lived isolated within our own walls. None of us had any notion, for example, of how the working class lived, despite huge worker protests that had shaken the country that year. The same applied to the 1870 war, which again didn't seem to touch us. Nor the crash of 1873. None of it concerned us, convinced as we were that the world outside remained in place. We were blissfully unaware that new forces were in fact undermining that edifice, and that a few decades later it would totally crumble.

Like most little children, I only cared about my immediate needs, and those close to me. I couldn't understand why we had left our old house in Hamburg, where I had been so happy. Why was my mother's face always somber? I wondered, and why did she always rail against Viennese education, the city's dirt, its ridiculous language, even against my father? I was of course too young to have been told that we had left Hamburg because my parents were running away from bankruptcy and my father's potential imprisonment.

My mother always detested Vienna, and as soon as she

could she fled back to Wandsbeck, a town outside Hamburg, where she lived close to her brother Elias. Her heart had remained attached to her country, Germany, especially the northern region where her family had lived for generations. She also missed Isaac Bernays, the sage, her father-in-law, the famous rabbi she adored and whose memory remained vivid long after his death. His presence was huge in our family, and whenever we ate in the dining room his portrait stared down, doubtless in judgment at us. Practicing believers, we lived in my grandfather's reflected glory. I found him handsome, with his long face, his high forehead under his black yarmulke, his big black eyes, and his provocative, sensual mouth. Clean-shaven except for a thin beard that gave a kind of blue shadow to his jaw, he carried himself severely erect, but nonetheless he had about him a soothing air of harmony. My grandfather didn't resemble any of the other rabbis I had seen in Leopoldstadt, with their traditional long black overcoats, thick long beards, and wide black hats. At first glance, with the two folded sides of his robe, he looked more like a pastor than a Middle European rabbi.

He didn't follow the kind of reformed Judaism prevalent in Germany at that time. Deriving from The Light, reformed Judaism distanced itself as much as possible from Christianity, especially Protestantism—which, in Prussia was the leading sect. What had made him famous in Wandsbeck was the originality of his teachings. His method was orthodox without any of the archaic trappings, and speaking German he was able to spread rigorous traditions. All of this was very appealing. You must remember that in the second half of the nineteenth century, Jews were sincerely happy living in Germany, proud to be sharing a refined culture, one they considered the height of civilization. Many Jews, in fact, felt so at home in Germany that they integrated further by converting, leaving behind all previous traditions. My father's younger brother Michael, after converting, went on to a brilliant academic career as a literature professor in Munich, where Ludwig II created a special chair for him. You can well imagine how that dishonorable act sat in my family. How could the son of Rabbi Bernays have committed such treason! His conversion was so intolerable to them that they pretended he had died, and never uttered his name again. The other son, my uncle Jakob, not only did not convert but remained faithful to his religion. He too enjoyed a successful academic career, as philosophy professor at the Jewish theological university of Breslau. As for my father, he kept to his faith throughout his life.

Like all German Jews, my parents went through life proud of who they were. There is a funny French expression, "Happy like God in France!" which could well apply to the Jews in Germany.

I learned early on about the hierarchy among European Jews. German Jews sat at the top of the pyramid. Toward the east and south there was poverty, absurd superstition, and a contemptible lack of culture—men in religious garb and long beards. I remember the shame Eastern Jews suffered, along with Galician Jews. When my mother called someone "Galizianer," it was a supreme insult.

For generations both sides of my family had been ensconced in Germany. On my mother's paternal side, however, there were the Philipps, who came from Sweden. And

I always relished that exotic side of my family, especially as I listened to my mother, who now and then broke into Swedish with her sister.

It is late and raining outside. The only noise I can hear is the drops of rain falling onto the garden, and occasionally little squeaky noises emanating from some furniture. Amusing how even furniture seems to have a mysterious life. There I go, rambling again. Do forgive me.

You had asked about Anna, Minna, and the year 1896, and here I am, evoking my early life. Strange . . . these fragmented thoughts surprise me, given my usual clear and orderly mind.

I must go now. Uncovering the past wears me out. I hope you won't mind the digression.

With affection as always,

Martha F.

6

The weather has turned very cold, with a kind of icy, relentless rain that keeps me indoors. Perfectly normal for this time of year, Peggy and Sophie assure me. On All Saints' Day, even the sky is in mourning. I hear giggles and soft chitchat downstairs, coming from the little English girls who, against my better judgment, have come to give Paula a hand. "I can take care of everything," she had insisted. "I don't need anyone else." I paid no heed to her, and am glad I hired them anyway. Their sweet presence pleases me, bringing in life and brightening the house. It is so important for me to feel life around me, especially since my last letter to Mary. I should have left those faraway memories to lie dormant, rather than unearthing the past, as I have done. Now they haunt me. Even my puzzle no longer seems to distract me.

Eighteen ninety-six. Fifty years ago—a turning point in my life. The kind where one follows irrevocably one direction rather than another. I don't know why I keep thinking about it. There were others, surely. The first and most important was without doubt that April evening of 1882 when a twenty six-year-old man looked at me intensely with his dark eyes—thus taking possession of my life. Or was it earlier, when I put my foot down to an arranged marriage? If I had accepted, I would obviously be in another place today, and not the wife of a famous man. How would my life have turned out? This kind of imagining is a treacherous game, and mere conjecture. As for me, I honestly feel that my life was preordained. I was ready and well prepared to become a model wife—one ready to accept what others might not have tolerated.

I have thought about it incessantly ever since my last letter. Reliving the moment when Minna first moved in with us and settled in the room next to ours, I am prey to a nagging question: Whose idea had it been in the first place? Could we have proceeded differently? Trying to project back to the layout of our apartment, I come to the conclusion—which undoubtedly is what obtained then—that that room next to ours was the only spot available in the house for Minna. No other member of our household could have occupied this spot. The maids? We certainly could not have allowed any of them to cross our room. The children? Absolutely not. It clearly was the only solution. No one seemed to object, or see anything troubling or abnormal about the situation. Except me. And I decided to keep it to myself. One white snowy afternoon, my sister arrived with all her belongings. Still tired from having given birth three weeks before, I watched in a daze as she unpacked, giving harsh orders to the bewildered maid, who had never before been spoken to in that peremptory manner. Breathing a sigh of relief when she had finished getting settled, Minna let herself fall into an easy chair as if to say, "Home at last!"

For months, I could hear every noise Minna made as she moved about in her room. When she went to bed, it was a creaking noise; when she moved the washbasin, I could hear the water splashing, as well as a myriad of other noises. I was of course painfully aware that she in turn could hear our every move, and I remember making sure to walk only on our rug and to quietly close our door.

In those days, Sigi never came up to bed at the same time as I did. He often stayed down to play cards with Minna after supper, and would subsequently retire to his office, where he would read or do some writing, doubtless to Wilhelm. Or work on his research. Page after page darkened with his nervous handwriting, destined for Fliess. How I loved his handwriting! While we were engaged, the first thing I used to do when mail arrived in Wandsbeck was to spot his handwriting, always leaning to the right, with its beautifully designed *f* or *h*. Now it was Wilhelm who had become the beneficiary of his wonderful letters while I went up to bed alone, usually at the same time my sister did.

I always tried to stay awake until Sigmund came up, but inevitably I fell asleep. I had expected — as had been the case after all my previous births—that as soon as I was myself again after Anna's birth, our marital life would resume, and things would revert to normal. I was wrong. That aspect of our life was definitely over. I had no longer any reason to worry about Minna's nocturnal proximity. As we spent our nights like good children, lying chastely next to each other, I resigned myself. The man who had once been my lover, my husband, was now neutral, devoid of sexuality, a good friend, a brother, the only difference being that my brother of course would not have slept in the same room. In any event, this sudden change in our relationship upset me greatly, but I didn't dare mention it to anyone. Both Minna and Sigmund acted as if everything was normal, and I soon felt silly for having harbored such malevolent thoughts. What's more, the baby my sister had presumably come to help me take care of—and who had separated Sigi and me—had quickly become his favorite child. Why, I had no idea. In any case, our life together had lost its harmony. Had that harmony been an illusion on my part? Did I fantasize it merely to convince myself I was a loved woman?

Be that as it may, these were the auspices under which the year began. As months went by, no one noticed that I had fallen into a morose silence. Meanwhile Minna had taken charge of the house, and I could hear her sonorous voice ordering the flustered domestics around. What she managed to do, however, was create complete chaos, leaving me to trail behind her picking up the pieces, as best I could. Looking doe-eyed at Sigmund, she spent her time exchanging witty remarks with him, not to mention monopolizing our dinner conversations about subjects she was fully aware I knew little or nothing about. Deeply preoccupied by his work, Sigmund was, as expected, oblivious to my feelings. Looking back, and given the depth of my depression then, I can't imagine how I managed to function in this apartment of ours, filled with children, nannies, and staff of one kind or other. But I did. Days rolled by with what would have appeared to anyone looking on, a jolly routine.

When summer came, I was on the verge of a nervous breakdown. School holidays were upon us, and as always, I was responsible for organizing everything down to the last detail. The women and children were to leave Vienna at the beginning of July, and Sigi was to join us early in August. In September, the plan was for Sigmund to go on and visit Wilhelm. All of a sudden, I was overwhelmed with a desire to get away, at least for a few days, from Sigmund, Minna, and the children.

*   *   *

There was but one place for me to turn: Wandsbeck, the house where my mother had lived since she retired thirteen years before. All I needed to invoke was fatigue—a normal state after my six pregnancies. A minor illness on my mother's part, mostly invented by me, seemed an honorable excuse for my departure. Sigmund's deep sense of family—his, mainly—helped. Of course I should go if my mother needed help! He was pleased at the thought of seeing his friend Wilhelm; I am not sure he really cared whether I was there or not. As for Minna, all she wanted was to run the house by herself. Everything seemed to work well for everyone. In early September, I left without any difficulty.

Looking back, I find my desire to visit my mother a bit odd. We weren't close, and I had never confided in her. My mother systematically discouraged confidence of any kind—she herself had never confided in anyone. So why then did I decide to go there? Maybe all I wanted was to return to the place of my youth, to a time before I was married. The last three years of my engagement were spent peacefully in that little brick house secluded in its garden, except for the few emotional storms Sigmund provoked. Did I have the illusion that, once back in my childhood home, I could start over again from scratch, erase the past, and print a new page in its place?

Pure illusion. This said, I have no regrets. Going home gave me the opportunity to discover another side of my mother.

In fact, returning to Wandsbeck filled me with great comfort. Everything was just as I had remembered, including grouchy Maria, the old maid. As for my mother, in her black dress, her braids tied neatly on top of her head, her hands folded on her lap, she was quietly waiting for me.

No sooner had I set foot in the house than she noticed something was troubling me. But as mothers will, she waited until I got settled to talk to me. As I reappeared, looking me straight in the eye, she asked: "So what's wrong?" To my utter surprise, I broke into an unexpected sob. I had not cried for years. What was happening? I wasn't sad. At least, I didn't think I was. It was nothing, surely. My mother pulled me to her. What did I do then? I sobbed even louder! Here was this woman, so cold and distant when I was growing up, over-whelming me with tenderness that was clearly heartfelt.

Gently taking me outside, she sat us down under the fragrant linden tree, and I began to talk. She listened to me for hours, her hand holding mine.

Things turned out so differently from what I had expected. That day I felt that my mother was the only one in whom I could confide. Why was I so unhappy? To have had six children was no reason to be unhappy. On the contrary. And all six were in fine shape. What was my problem, then? Sigi? Wasn't he a perfect husband? He was a genius, worked hard, was faithful, didn't drink or gamble, and loved his children. Was it his work? But wasn't it normal for a man to work hard and be ambitious? Surely, I could not wish for a husband who stayed home doing nothing. No, Sigmund spent all his effort and energy earning a living for his family, as well as improving the lot of his patients.

My mother was quietly listening to me as I supplied answers to my own questions, staring at the ivy on the brick wall in front of us. "What is wrong with you?" she repeated. I was taken aback by her direct question. I had no idea what was wrong. Was it because Sigi no longer noticed me? Or that I had become a mere object—an important one, perhaps, but nonetheless an object—to him? That was it! I had touched upon the truth: I counted as much as all the others, not one iota more than Wilhelm or Minna. While we all had our roles to play, mine had no more value in Sigi's eyes than did the others. I didn't exist—for anyone—was my conclusion.

"I always wondered whether Minna's arrival in your house was such a good idea!" my mother muttered, emerging from her silence.

And all of a sudden it all came out. My jealousy, my feelings of having been abandoned, all sorts of complaints and recriminations, came bursting forth. Why had Sigmund relegated me to the role of housewife, incapable of assisting him like Minna? I too had had a fine education, spoke good German, was sensitive to writers' styles. I could have understood as well as Minna what he spoke about—had he only cared to share his thoughts. No. From the start, I knew Sigmund had precisely cast me in the role of mother, hausfrau, someone from whom he expected comfort and peace. Nothing more.

During our engagement, Sigmund had already clearly charted how he perceived the role of a wife. He didn't agree with John Stuart Mill, who in his book advocated equality of sexes. If a wife of his were to be working, Sigmund would discourage her at once, considering her to be competition. He would implore her to quit, asking her to take refuge—I remember vividly his words—"in the calm activity—where there would be no competition—of her home." Nature had seen to it that by giving woman beauty, charm, and affection, Sigmund declared. I therefore fulfilled the role he had designed for me, that of a delicate creature who needed his protection.

In those days, nothing in me suggested I revolt. None of the feminist theses had reached me, unlike my friend Bertha Pappenheim. I would have continued playing that role—with the sole aim of pleasing him—had Sigmund only bothered to notice that something had gotten lost since our marriage. I am referring to that intangible spice that had peppered our engagement, and had fed my hopes—his declarations of love, his confidences. The deep conversations that had filled our correspondence had led me to believe our future life together would be a rich one. Sigmund had no clue that the loss of all that had left me desolate, in complete isolation. Of course, surrounded as I was by children, domestics, members of the family, and assured of my husband's presence and faithfulness, I should have been filled with satisfaction. I realized then, speaking to my mother, that what was essential to my life was missing.

What had been most difficult was having to keep my frustrations to myself. I had not earned the right to complain, and no one would have understood me if I had. Meanwhile, Sigmund was no longer confiding in me; that was a fact. From then on, whatever preoccupied him—disappointments or pain—was shared with others. But how was he to see that I was hurt? In my husband's eyes, I was as solid as a rock. He needed the rock to lean on. I gave him his perfect wife, his perfect mother. Weren't we, in the eyes of everyone, an ideal family?

I could no longer go on with this charade. I had reached my limits.

In a reaction that stunned me, my mother burst out

laughing. How could she laugh, after the painful things I just had told her? "I'm not making fun of you," she said, taking my arm. "What amuses me is hearing you say that your atheist husband is behaving exactly like the most Orthodox man. You can't have forgotten, I am sure, that that is precisely what Talmudists demand: a wife must do everything in her power to help her husband study. I have no idea what he is studying, but it must have the same value for him as it does for any bearded Talmudist." Looking at me sweetly, she wiped a tear from my cheek.

The emotions I felt then, and still feel today, prevent me from writing further. It isn't so much what I had confessed to my mother—I have long since buried it all, and none of it pains me any longer—it's the memory of my mother's utter kindness, and how close I felt to her then, really for the first time. Nostalgia overwhelmed me. I saw little of her during the remaining fourteen years of her life. I had sacrificed her to Sigmund, who hated her from the very beginning. Was it, on his part, a desire to own me entirely, without any competition? Or was it that my mother lacked the unconditional worship he had enjoyed from his own mother? It's true that my mother was quick to criticize him. That infuriated him. From the time we were engaged, he did his best to distance me from her, accusing her of being selfish, bossy, and insufferably blind to her religion. Sigmund counted on my sharing his feelings about my mother. While in most things I had abdicated my own opinion to espouse his, early on in our relationship I managed to resist this one. That day in Wandsbeck, I understood how right I had been.

*   *   *

The following days were spent accompanying my mother on various errands, and tending her ever so meticulous garden, with its perfect rows, devoid of any weeds—I had forgotten to what degree order was key to her life. A new kind of self-examination preoccupied me. I slept little at night, listening to silence, consumed with trying to dredge up long-buried memories. During our long walks together in the woods, I felt how much her soothing presence meant to me. The serenity that emanated from her made me feel at peace, as if I was a lake surrounded by tall mountains. During one of these walks, my mother began to talk about herself, something she had never done before.

"You know, my dear, it's not as though life has been all that easy for me. Like you, I married young, full of illusions, without the slightest notion of what lay in store for me. Like you, I believed marriage was the beginning of true happiness. Mine was an arranged marriage. I hardly knew the man I was marrying, but I didn't dislike him, and he inspired confidence in me. It seemed a good thing. Both our families were honorable, and the thought of becoming daughter-in-law to famous Rabbi Bernays—someone I greatly admired—pleased me to no end. Had it been allowed for girls in those days, I would have loved to study with him. Your father and I got along well. He was a good man. Our life, however, was far from what I had anticipated. He was absorbed by his work and all its problems. We very quickly fell into our own respective routines. It was the same for all the other families. I accepted it as normal: I was swallowed up by domestic duties of house and family, he in the throes of his work life. However, because of him, I was reduced to living in poverty, even dishonor. For reasons I won't go into, he had to declare bankruptcy, was arrested, and served time in prison for debts! You simply have no idea how humiliating this is if you are part of a small community. Furthermore, three of our children died not long after they were born. We had had time to name each child, see their first smiles. No sooner had I become emotionally involved with each one than he was taken away, leaving me heartbroken and bereft. When your little Mathilde fell ill, I was worried the same would happen

"These were extremely painful and difficult days. I can't imagine where I found the strength to go on. Your father was of no help, incapable of expressing feelings or even communicating. As for me, I was too proud to complain. We each kept our frustrations to ourselves. My three surviving children, and my faith, were what kept me going. I could have harbored anger and railed against God for the cruelty he had inflicted on us. I felt grateful He hadn't abandoned me. Every time I felt despair, I recited to myself David's psalm, the one you must recall: 'The Lord is my Shepherd, I shall not want.' Today He has granted me a peaceful old age, and my family is not far from me. No persecution has plagued me. I say grace to Him every day."

Coming from my mother, these confessions moved me greatly. I also understood her message clearly. But I was pleased that for the first time in her life she could talk about herself.

I too had to move on and fulfill the duties expected of me. Unlike her, however, there was no faith to help me. While I questioned whether I had ever had faith, I did not share my husband's atheism, which seemed filled with hate. Man had to have something other than reason. There had to be something else. What I learned from listening to my mother that day was very important: I had to stop expecting the impossible. No one was going to hand me my destiny on a silver platter. I needed to take charge of it. By myself. Also, I wanted in a way to emulate her and make her proud of me.

The next day, I felt as though the sky had lifted. We both chatted and gossiped about a number of people. She told me about a young friend of hers, Magda, whose husband, a certain Kadish, had just died. With time, she could envisage her remarrying, my mother said; she was young and well off financially.

In an instant I was back in 1881, fifteen years earlier. I was twenty, and the only thing important for me then was finding a husband. A wealthy neighbor—a distinguished member of my mother's synagogue, and whose lavish wardrobe and lifestyle my mother admired—stopped in for a visit with an interesting proposition. A widower friend of hers had noticed me. My youth, good manners, and reserved appearance had apparently seduced him. His name was Hugo Kadish. He had two grown children. With such a catch, she went on, there would be no concern about a dowry. This Mr. Kadish was rich, had a large apartment on the Ring; my future was assured. I would have everything a woman could dream of. Another favorable point, she added—he was a German Jew, from Cologne, and had everything going for him, including being a good practicing man, a mensch well respected in his community. Would my mother agree to meeting with him?

A few days later I found myself accompanied by my mother and Minna to that friendly woman's apartment, with its velvet drapes, lace, and a myriad of bric-a-brac everywhere. When she received us, it was obvious she was enjoying her role of marrying agent. The gentleman in question was already there when we arrived. Well dressed, with an air of someone accustomed to wealth and comfort, he was rather corpulent, and could pass for my father. All in all, though, I didn't find him unattractive, as I had feared I would. We were served tea and pastries on fine Meissen china, and our conversation ran smoothly over this and that. Mr. Kadish was respectful as he addressed my mother, and asked thoughtful questions about me. Being on exhibit, like a horse at a fair, made me increasingly uncomfortable. I felt confused and a bit shaken as we took our leave. What did I think of Mr. Kadish? asked my mother. I remained silent. I knew full well that if I married that man, all my family problems would be solved. No, I didn't find him unpleasant. And the notion that my sacrifice would save my parents' situation was obviously appealing to me. An arranged marriage? That was the furthest thing from my mind. I was dreaming of true love. And wasn't Mr. Kadish far too old, anyway?

Several days later our good neighbor came back, this time armed with a formal marriage proposal. Mr. Kadish really liked me. He would indeed marry me without dowry, and would be generous with my family, which he knew was in need. My mother was perfect: without a comment she passed the message to me.

I didn't refuse right off the bat; I thanked her and asked for time to think about it. Minna shrugged her shoulders contemptuously. "Why in the world would you even consider taking care of someone else's children, who would automatically detest you and make your life hell? Everyone knows how people view stepmothers!" were the words she filled my ears with.

Eli, my brother, came to the rescue. "It'll be for the rest of your life, can't you see? You'll have to share all. Haven't you thought of that?"

No, I had not. But as I did, for the first time, a cold shiver went up my spine.

"If it's for the money, don't give it another thought. I'm here for you. I can't bear the idea that you would bypass the most wonderful thing in the world—love—for pure material reasons."

Charged with my wonderful brother's ammunition, I announced my decision to my mother, who took it without a reproach. I saw from the wrinkles on her forehead, however, that I had left her pensive and worried.

"Do you believe I would have been happy with him, as a husband?" I asked her.

With a serious expression on her face, she replied, "I'm not sure. No, I don't believe you would have been. In fact, knowing you, you would have been miserable. Still, he was a man of many qualities, not to mention that you would never have had any money worries. His wife had nothing but good things to say about him. Marrying him would have been a reasonable solution . . . and aren't you reasonable?"

"But I didn't love him!"

"Love! My dear child, men and women are here to found families. Yes, one does in the best of all possible worlds need a bit of love for all that. But I really don't think men and women are fundamentally made to get along. Also, time wears love down. Intrinsically different, men and women have an entirely opposite view of love. Women dream to be one with the man they love; men, once romance has left, insist that their women fulfill their marital obligations, and regard them at best with affection. But basically, they live their life outside the home. Other interests hold their attention, starting with their career. Of course, at times, other women come into play. How can women not be disappointed? That is why you would surely have come to appreciate Mr. Kadish. Maybe even as much as you do Sigmund. But all this is a moot point. One can't rewrite history. You chose another road, and now, you must follow it."

After ten days, she kindly suggested I leave.

"Time to return home. Your children need you."

I would have gladly stayed longer, but feeling restored, I agreed to go. I had changed in a way I could not really pinpoint. But having discovered an ally full of wisdom and love in my mother made me go in peace. It had been an important discovery.

Back home, everyone expressed the hope that my mother was feeling better now, and things quickly fell back into place. Life resumed as before.

7

Dear Mary,

Calling you by your first name, as you have requested, doesn't come easy for me — a woman of an old Europe full of traditions and protocols. I am constantly shocked when my American friends, no doubt out of some feeling of affection, call *me* by my first name. I would much rather be called Frau Professor by those who are not my family. It is different with you. You could easily be my daughter, even my granddaughter. I actually marvel at how quickly we have become so familiar with one another.

Thank you for being so understanding when I seem to digress and ramble on about all kinds of unrelated things. Once one opens the paths of memory, there's no telling what emerges. I certainly don't seem to have much control. You are familiar with the process, I am sure, having been analyzed. Thank you for encouraging my free train of thought; it makes it easier for me to open up. Have you ever considered becoming my analyst? I must confess that idea is not displeasing.

Could it be the reason for last night's dream? It has been quite a while since I welcomed this nocturnal messenger.

Anyway, I was in my childhood apartment in Hamburg. A northern light, brilliant and white, with a trace of fog, was lighting us.

My mother—or was it Anna?—stood in front of me, looking strict, about to reproach me for some error I had committed. I didn't know what it was. I was looking for help from my brother Eli, whose back was turned to me, so he didn't see my distress. I became frightened. I had never experienced that light anywhere else. Evoking my Hamburg apartment and my mother always fills me with nostalgia as I wake up, even when it brings with it some fear or worry. What am I supposed to feel guilty about? I wonder. Writing to you? It is true that there is an aura of secrecy around our letter writing. I make sure to hide any trace of our correspondence. I write you furtively late at night, and I go to the post office myself to mail my letters. As for your letters, I hope you'll forgive me, I burn them as soon as I have read them.

Haunted by the thought of dying, I know there is no place where those letters couldn't be found. I beg you to do the same, on your end. While I fully trust you, I shudder at the thought of my letters falling into a stranger's hands.

Maybe the fact of having written you about my childhood in Hamburg, remembering my mother, triggered that dream of mine. Mother was calm, not inclined to show her emotions, which led some people to think her cold. I wanted to please her, and probably even emulate some of her mannerisms. For me she was a model. I found her beautiful. She had an imposing presence although she was small, and what always impressed me was her natural sense of authority. I remember trying hard to imitate the way she parted her hair in the middle, until I learned that as a pious young married woman, she was wearing a wig, which I would have to do, once I was married. Although that notion repelled me, I knew I too would have to cut my long hair and wear the *sheitel*. Or, like some women around me, maybe tie a scarf around my head. Well, it all turned out differently. I bent to other demands.

Every religious law was respected in our home. My mother saw to that. We ate kosher, rested Saturdays, attended services at the synagogue for all the holy celebrations. Friday evenings, she lit candles as she hid her face and whispered benediction. Following what she had been initiated into, she participated in the mystery I wanted so much to understand.

My father remains a distant character of my childhood. I find it difficult to tell you much about him. I knew he never held any intellectual profession, and next to his two brilliant brothers, he seemed rather pale. He worked selling lingerie, which always embarrassed me, I remember. Subsequently he dabbled in the stock market, which soon brought him to bankruptcy—and our shame. I don't remember much about the year he spent in jail. It is curious, you noted, that I should show so little emotion about an event that at the time brought us so much shame. Perhaps it's because I only learned about it later, after his death. My mother never brought it up, and I preferred to forget it. In Vienna, he took a job as secretary for a well-known economist, Lorenz von Stein, then later became editor of a newsletter specializing in train and steamship travel—certainly not literary, but to me it was still better than selling lingerie. None of this made any apparent impression on my mother, who always behaved like a proper wife no matter what the family's problems. But I could see there was no love lost for him. In retrospect, I feel sad that I never got to know him. I should have tried meeting him halfway, but I did not, this fallen man, this humiliated father of mine.

When I share with you the difficulties my own sons experienced as the children of a very famous father, I think that, in a way, theirs was not dissimilar to my own family's experience. My grandfather's crushingly tough image had its effect on his sons. My uncle Michael's way of fighting it was to convert to Christianity. Imagine, the son of a famous rabbi! If one of our sons had become a Jungian, it would have had the same impact in our house. As for my father, he never got out from under his business failures, his bankruptcy, accusations of fraud, and finally, the shame of prison. These had to be direct offences to the sage and irreproachable man his father was. Not to mention my mother: Had she married him so she could bear his famous father's name? I often wondered.

It was my mother who most of the time evoked my grandfather. She named my brother Isaak after him. He was six years older than me, and in good pious families boys were educated separately from the women. I knew he was a model student at the Talmudic school and respected all the rules of our religion. My mother seemed to prefer him. She may have hoped he would become his grandfather's reincarnation, or better yet, his successor. But Isaak was fragile, pale, and thin. His long days of studies didn't help matters. He became very ill as soon as he reached adolescence. Whispers of tuberculosis of the bones were heard. I had no idea what that meant. I remember seeing him hobbling on two crutches, pale, and then later, flat on his back, his face transparent. He declined rapidly, suffering greatly, and died at the age of seventeen. We were living in Vienna at the time, and I was eleven.

Thankfully, my other brother, Eli, who was only a year older than me, was there. I loved him dearly. Despite our separate educations, we managed to stay quite close. Not an intellectual like his brother, Eli radiated happiness. His keen practical sense perhaps brought us close. Minna was more like Isaak. People said she was very intelligent, like him. But in those days, in middle-class families, being an intelligent woman was inconsequential. Intelligence was reserved for men. "Women have no business walking on men's territory," my mother's peers said. This of course was precisely what put Minna in a state of perpetual revolt.

It was only years later that I learned about the death of my other three siblings: Fabien, Michael, and Sarah, who were born between Isaak and Eli. My mother made a point of never talking about them, just as she hid her true feelings about Isaak's death. When I discovered many years later how much she had suffered from all these deaths, I got a glimpse of that sad, secret aspect of her life and understood why her face so often wore a dark veil of gravity.

After my father died, we had serious financial problems. My mother's dowry had long evaporated into my father's abortive businesses. The kitty was empty. Begging for help from her relatives was out of the question. Eli came to her rescue by picking up where our father had left off. Immediately taking the helm of my father's business, he turned it around and made a profit. Her savior, he suddenly took Isaak's place in her heart. From then on, it was him she talked to, and him she relied upon.

Images of Rembrandtstrasse, in Vienna, where we lived until 1883, came flooding back to me. Our life now, under my mother's tutelage, fell back into its Hamburg routine. She had seen to it that our furniture resumed its familiar place, reminiscent of our previous abode, including the rabbi's portrait, which, as it had before, hung in our new dining room. We went every day with our maid to a beautiful garden near where we lived, the Augarten. Not far from us, about a mile away, was the Prater, where we would all go on special occasions. I used to enjoy these outings; they gave me a glimpse of a whole other society, unknown to me, brilliant and lively. There I saw for the first time the Viennese strolling: military men in their dress uniforms, elegant ladies walking under their umbrellas, gentlemen with shiny top hats. Café terraces, where live music was played, were filled with people enjoying lives. I was awed by it all. It was all in such contrast to our own austere lives. Like my siblings, I took mental notes of this spectacle, and always returned home overwhelmed by this universe I was discovering.

I entered a small school for girls under Miss Wertenschlag—a spinster with a mole on her chin and thick black eyebrows—where I soon made a few girlfriends who remained my friends well into adulthood. My brothers went to a boys school, and Isaak added to his curriculum studies in a Talmudic school.

I still remember with fondness our new maid Gretl, who came to live with us. She was young, blond, and always in a good mood. The way she rolled her *r*'s (in the Viennese manner) was a constant source of amusement. Instructed to accompany us everywhere for some fresh air—mostly the garden nearby—she ventured with us to Donaukanal, unbeknownst to my mother, and showed us the old city. A fervent Catholic, she took us to visit churches: Stephankirche,

Schottenkirche, and Peterkirche. We learned all sorts of new things: how to dip our finger in holy water, make the sign of the cross, kneel in the pew, hold our hands tightly together, and look serious. Each time, as we left a church, I remember feeling terrified. First, there was the feeling of having betrayed my mother's teachings, and too, I couldn't help being paranoid, dreadfully worried that people, discovering we were Jews, would throw us ignominiously out of their superb edifices. Meanwhile, each church's rich decorations, with so much gold and art in every corner, made me realize how bare and austere our prayer rooms were by comparison.

Gretl also took us a few times to the Ring, where every day one could glimpse the finest Vienna society had to offer. Each afternoon, social and political celebrities could be seen strolling back and forth along the few hundred yards separating it from Schwartzenberd Square. She would point out to us this minister, that famous opera singer, or this courtesan. We would return home from these exciting outings—where we had experienced entirely new vistas and people—exhausted but energized. We knew how to keep our lips sealed, though. I remember dreaming about these extraordinary outings. Today, what remains of them in my memory are mostly fun and positive images.

Gretl was precious to me. She kept me informed about what was happening in the world, things my mother was ignorant of or had turned her back on. Through her, I learned details of Viennese society and the part Jews played in it. Everything was arranged in concentric circles, starting with the imperial family. Knowing that Emperor Franz-Joseph's palace was near was magical to me, recalling the fairy tales I used to read when I was a child. From where we stood, we could see the walls of the Hofburg palace. The notion that there, only a few yards away, the emperor was sitting at his desk, immersed in some important task, always impressed me. All his portraits showed his reassuring corpulence, his thick sideburns, making him resemble our grandfather. He would get up at four each morning, Gretl informed us, and often put in a thirteen-hour day. All this for his people! she would exclaim. Hating to linger at table, even at official dinners, the emperor would gobble down his twelve courses in less than half an hour, forcing his guests to do the same.

She also regaled us girls with tales of the grand court balls. There was the Ball bei Hof—reserved for the aristocracy—and the Hofball, to which second-tier aristocrats were invited. Dazzling us further, she gave us minute descriptions of the jewelry, long beautiful gowns, and shiny uniforms, and showed us how they all waltzed. Needless to say, each night I would fall asleep reliving these glitzy soirees.

I learned that the emperor's wife, Elizabeth—whom Gretl called Sissi, as all the Viennese did—was beautiful. Gretl showed me portraits of her wearing an extraordinarily pretty gown—a kind I had never seen, with bare shoulders. Again and again, I would ask Gretl to show it to me just once more.

None of this was of any interest to Mother. She never stopped telling us that we had no business with the world of goyim! Our kingdom was deep studies, decency, and piety—none of the superficial accoutrements of the big world, which could only lead to debauchery. Talking to Mother about Sissi's portrait, with her bare shoulders and the outrageous luxury of her magnificent gown, was simply out of the question. I kept it my big secret! Later on, as Minna grew up, I attempted to share my awe with her. But her response was unenthusiastic, to say the least. "How can you admire Sissi when all she has is what she was born with? She does not merit any of it!" Minna said.

In 1873, things changed completely. Following Isaak's illness, which had absorbed all our mother's time, and after Gretl had become her temporary surrogate, my mother once again took charge of our education. When she learned of our escapades with Gretl, the maid was summarily dismissed. I was devastated. Replacing Gretl, a grim, thin-lipped Moravian maid who never smiled arrived. Gone was the fun. My grooming for a future perfect hausfrau had begun.

I was about to become a woman, and my mother issued strict orders that from then on I was to avoid contact with men at all cost. I was to keep secret and private any vestige of bleeding—especially from my brothers and father. She proceeded to instruct me on how to deal with the new phenomenon. Frightened, I became more reserved and afraid than ever. Each afternoon, upon returning from school, I was taught how to cook kosher, according to our religious rules, how to sew, how to run a household in general. Like my mother, I too would use two different sets of dishes. "Make sure you never cook kid goat in its mother's milk!" she told me. She listed the thousand and one other things forbidden me. There was no question in her mind that I would follow and respect tradition. In no way did I question any of her prescriptions. Gone were my earlier dreams. I was on my way to becoming, like her, a proper, virtuous, devoted wife.

Why would a man ever choose me? I kept wondering,

as I grew older. I was aware that it had become imperative for me to bring something concrete home, given the state of our finances. If I didn't marry, what did the future hold for me? Would I be a governess? A lady's companion? We had to wait until 1897 for women to be allowed to attend a university. And even then, literature was the only educational possibility for women. It took three more years for women to be allowed to enter medical school. But only a scant few girls had the nerve to break tradition. In rich milieus, it was actually a stigma for a woman to work.

That a woman's fate was preordained in those days didn't seem to trouble me. I sincerely aspired to follow my mother's example. What did concern me was the thought of having to marry a man who repelled me. As I viewed the men around me, brothers or cousins of girlfriends of mine, they were all grotesque in one way or other: I found them ugly. I shuddered at the very idea of having to marry any of them!

In our home, no feminine coquetry was permitted. I wore my hair parted in the middle and pulled back in a tight chignon, which accentuated the severity of my looks. My wardrobe consisted of utterly plain clothes, buttoned high at the neck, with sleeves neatly covering my arms. In summertime, dresses of light-colored, flowered fabric were the only frivolity allowed.

Only when I met Sigmund did I overcome my lack of self-confidence. You have undoubtedly noticed, Mary, there is nothing like being loved to restore your self-confidence. Many years later, well into my marriage, when my husband left for long periods, some of my old anxieties and self-doubt crept back. In fact, by 1896 I had in large measure reverted to my old lack of self-esteem. I never showed it, of course. To those around me, I displayed the smooth mask of the content, perfectly happy housewife.

When summer came, I would plan our vacation trips in detail—an inconceivable endeavor for the Bernays. But for Sigi, I knew that summer break was imperative. The only trips we would take when I was growing up in Hamburg were to visit my uncle Elias in Wandsbeck, or my aunt Lea. Renting summer houses, staying in hotels, or going to spas was scorned as frivolous. For the Freud family, on the contrary, hardly richer than ours had been, no summer was complete without a vacation trip. Our meager savings were spent each year for those vacations.

To escape the heat, we did as every other Viennese family did: we left the city. The children and I would leave Vienna in June, and Sigmund would join us at the end of July. Our departures were veritable expeditions, obliging me to book two train compartments to accommodate all eight of us, plus our maids. I don't remember why, but we always seemed to travel with an enormous amount of linen, clothes, books, and other apparently necessary objects. One thing was sure: Sigi needed to feel comfortable, and I saw to that by organizing those trips in minute detail, almost as if we were actually moving. The children looked forward to those vacations, for these were the rare moments when their father really gave them his time. Taking them for long walks, he enjoyed teaching the children how to pick wild mushrooms. Even for us women, those vacations were a special, privileged time.

In the beginning, we would rent a house in Semmering, in Maria-Scutz. Later on, if we felt less flush, it was in Bellevue, an outskirt of Vienna. We would often go from there to visit my mother-in-law or various friends living nearby.

Sigmund adored walking, particularly taking excursions in the mountains. He always dreamed of really grand voyages. Only in 1895 were his dreams fulfilled. Sigmund was able to travel with his brother to Italy. Pregnant with Anna, I couldn't join them. We spent the following summer with Minna, who by then had become an integral part of our household, vacationing in Aussee, in Styria, after which I visited my mother in Wandsbeck. Sigmund was to meet Wilhelm in Salzburg, following which he would meet his brother Alexander in Venice. In fact, taking a trip alone at the end of each summer became a ritual for Sigmund. I was only able to accompany him twice. For the rest of the summer, Minna or Alexander became his companions. He and Minna went on long walking trips two years in a row, going through glaciers, over mountaintops, all of which Sigmund described in idyllic terms to me in his letters. I remember the summer of 1898, when they came to fetch me, asking me to join them in Dalmatia. Less proficient in the art of walking, I politely declined, so they continued on to Brescia, Milan, Bergamo. Sigi was indefatigable. So was Minna. After discovering Riemerlehen Farm in Berchtesgaden the following summer, Sigmund stopped taking his end-of-summer trips. That summer, he sat down to write his *Interpretation of Dreams*.

As the years went by, Bavaria became our place of choice for summer vacations. The house we rented was sufficiently large to accommodate everyone, including our domestics. We could have easily been taken for a perfect Austrian family—with our boys in leather pants, the girls in flowered dirndls with their square décolletés, and Sigmund always elegant in his sport suits, with good leather shoes and a Tyrolian hat—except for our children's eyes, so black, we were often asked whether we might be Italian. Needless to say, we made certain not to contradict that notion with the locals. The mere mention of being Jewish would have created a malaise, which we wanted to avoid at all costs. That didn't keep Sigmund from being harassed one day by a crowd of people as he was taking his daily walk. He was only able to chase them off by brandishing his cane menacingly.

That incident left a deep impression in me. Why weren't we part of this country, or of Germany, where we shared so much? "Das Wandern ist des Müllers Lust"—already expressing his love of nature, Sigmund used to sing this as a young child, like all the other Austrian children. Like Germans, we sometimes spoke the Austrians' language better than they. We too shared a taste for order, for decency. I couldn't fathom why they didn't accept us as theirs.

From that time on, my husband took to traveling alone every year in early September, without me or the children. Italy was his land of preference. Feeling a particular passion for Rome, he returned there regularly, starting in 1901. Sigmund also developed a keen eye for Greek and Roman antiquities, so that after each of his Italian trips, several little statuettes appeared to take their place in his collection. His letters or cards, addressed to the whole family, would arrive full of his enthusiasms. "Dear mother" or "Dear old girl!" was how he addressed me. What ever happened to "My dear beloved" or "My Princess"? At forty, had I become that old in his eyes?

Dear Mary, I must interrupt now. I need to regroup. I

had no idea how much joy these letters would bring me, nor how much hardship they would unleash at the same time. Do forgive me once again for going on about my childhood, and my early married life.

I send affectionate greetings to you,

Martha Freud

8

This November is definitely a grim one. Rain has kept me from my daily walks, and I miss them. The weather has been so bad, I had to ask Peggy to mail my letter, pleading with her to be discreet about it—I wonder whether my request might have seemed weird to her. "You didn't forget to mail my letter, did you?" I kept asking her when she returned. Offended, she looked at me oddly, concerned at my unusual nervousness.

Our correspondence has filled me with joy until now—I wouldn't stop it for the world—but I am unable to shake the many thoughts, memories, emotions it has provoked. It is as though a machine within me is churning, and I am unable to stop it.

"Your destiny is elsewhere," my mother would tell me. What did she mean? I often wondered. Did she mean it had all been set since my birth, somewhere, and all I needed to do was wait until it played out at the prescribed moment? Meeting Sigmund, I must say, almost made me believe her words.

At the end of April 1882, Minna and I were visiting my friend Mitzi Freud, in Kaiserhofstrasse. Mitzi and I had become fast friends ever since we met during my last year in Miss Wertenschlag's school. Both the same age, we got along immediately. Neither outshone the other; neither, for that matter, claimed to be any beauty prize. Rather short, Mitzi drew her hair neatly back in a long braid. Her happy nature radiated. We visited her in the dark apartment where she lived with her large family. Anna, the oldest of the girls, three years older than I, seemed haughty and pretentious and made a point of ignoring us. In short, I didn't take to her. Nor did her personality improve later on, after she married my brother Eli. On the other hand, I was crazy about the other girls, all of whom I found exceptionally nice. After Anna came Rosa, my friend Mitzi, Dolfi, and Pauli. Very close to one another, they all had in common a positive nature—everything and everybody always appeared fine to them. The pack of Freud girls seemed to follow one another in peaceful agreement, almost to the point where one wondered whether they weren't perhaps a bit simpleminded!

The youngest son, Alexander, like his sister Anna, never mingled with the rest of us. As for the oldest son, Sigmund, he was away at university, studying hard to become a doctor. "Sigmund will surely do great things," the sisters chimed in chorus. "He has to be a genius!" Anna, who had assumed the role of second mother to them, was orchestrating the chorus. A mere allusion to Sigi would bring honey to her mouth, and her eyes would shine. "My *Goldener* Sigi!" (My golden Sigi) one could hear her say time and again.

I recall finding the Freud parents rather exotic. Jacob, the father, seemed old to me when I first met them in 1880. At sixty-five, he was some twenty years older than his wife Amalia. Kind, with a soft and friendly disposition, he gave the impression of being tired, doubtless because of the prominent bags under the eyes. Always at home—he had stopped working—I saw him most of the time sitting happily in a big easy chair, reading or watching the goings-on of his many progeny. I recall being surprised when Mitzi told me that his older children—who were the age of his present wife—from an earlier marriage lived in Manchester, England.

What impressed me most was the mother's personality. So different from my mother's! I had assumed that all mothers were reserved, strict, and always dignified. This one moved about with great energy, was loud, and despite her rather messy style, exercised enormous authority over the entire family. My mother would have qualified her behavior as *Schlamperei*. But they all marched to her tune. She reigned with an iron hand over her little kingdom, to the unfettered admiration of her husband, who could not get over this lively and youthful wife of his.

It didn't take long for me to see she favored her eldest son. The girls, crowded into two small rooms, with the exception of Anna, all seemed content, whereas Sigmund enjoyed his own study next to the bedroom he shared with Alexander. What bothered Anna increasingly were two things: In order not to disturb Sigmund's studying, she had been forbidden to practice her piano; the other thing she couldn't tolerate was Sigmund's influence on his sisters' education, and the way he lectured them on what to read. Anna couldn't wait to marry and leave the house! she let everyone know. Crowded or not, the other sisters were only too pleased to conform to their mother's and older brother's wishes, parading their unequivocal adoration and attachment to their family.

When I first described the Freud family, my mother listened with a pinched expression. "The Freuds! I have heard of them," she replied. "But aren't they *Galizianer?*"

"Of course not!" I protested, fully aware that that was the worst insult in her eyes. "They came from Freiberg, in Moravia, and settled in Vienna ten years before," I hurried to inform her.

"Before Moravia they must have lived in Galicia," she retorted. "It's obvious when you look at the mother! I'm not so sure about the father. In any case, they are not real Germans! That's for certain!"

That said it all. How could one socialize with them? Were they practicing people? I had to admit they weren't, having noticed that the Freuds didn't respect Shabbat and, in fact to the best of my knowledge, never set foot inside a synagogue either. After considerable histrionics, I had to promise not to share any meals with "those people." In fact, I was to stop seeing them. Period. But I refused. Visiting them was my sole distraction, and no matter how strongly my mother disapproved, nothing would keep me from going to Kaiser-Josefstrasse. "Let your friend Mitzi come to our house! That's fine, I'll receive her here!" my mother offered. This calmed her, momentarily, and allowed me to continue seeing my friend.

One afternoon, as I sat eating apples in their dining room with Mitzi, Dolfi, Pauli, and Rosa, I heard the front door open, and a young dark-haired man with a thick beard entered the house. It was their brother Sigmund. I assumed he was merely passing through on his way to his room. However, after glancing inside the dining room and registering our presence, he entered and joined us, something he apparently never did. Normally, his sisters told me, he would arrive and immediately go to his room to study, either alone or with some fellow students. The knife with which I was peeling my apple remained poised in the air as he stood staring at me.

Sigmund later confided to me that that first glance was a decisive moment, a turning point for him. He was of course careful not to show any of this at the time. The French call it a *coup de foudre*—being thunderstruck; the Germans say *Liebe am ersten blick*, love at first sight. As for me, I can't say I fell the first moment I met Sigi. I found him nice enough, with good features, but relatively short. Too short, really, for my taste at the time. According to Minna, I blushed. His penetrating stare, and the strength he exuded, intimidated me. For me, love came later.

Whenever I visited his sisters, he would make a point of joining us, and each time, he fixed me with the same intense stare, embarrassing me and leaving me with a strange new sense of anticipation. He soon started speaking about himself in a kind of exalted tone, which left me astonished, even a little worried. I wasn't accustomed to so much passion. Research was what interested him, he said. He wanted to make a difference. When he asked me about myself, I answered with my usual shyness, and when I reported these conversations to Minna, her reaction was: "The doctor is awfully kind to be so interested in us!" What was that "us"? It irritated me. How did she manage to incorporate herself into this?

When Sigmund gave me a copy of *David Copperfield*— which we still have on our bookshelf—I baked him a cake as a thank-you. This was June 13. I had been invited to the Freuds'. That evening, Sigmund sat to my right at dinner, and the next thing I knew, he was squeezing my hand under the table, making my heart jump. That did it! It had all happened so fast, I let myself be taken by the whirlwind without resisting. Sigmund had achieved his victory over me without leaving me any time to breathe or think.

On June 15, I was to receive the first of the nine hundred and forty letters he wrote me during our engagement. It started in English—to this day I never knew why he wrote in English, "My sweet darling girl." I often remove that letter from the safe where I keep all the others, bound by different-colored ribbons, labeled by year. I read it over and over, and each time it is with tenderness mixed with a sense of the ridiculous. Knowing Sigmund's acute and incredible intelligence, his profound distaste for anything conventional, which at times made him seem hard and sarcastic, I can't help but wonder how in the world he could have written such purple prose—even in love, as he then was. Wasting no time, forty-eight hours after his first letter, we decided—his decision, no doubt—that that was the day of our engagement. It would remain our secret. I left the very next day for Wandsbeck for my long-planned vacation at my uncle Elias's house. We were to act as if no one knew, except Eli and Minna. How foolish. Everyone, including his sister, his parents, and my mother, of course, had noticed Sigmund's zealous behavior.

From the very beginning, Sigmund adopted an attitude of respect, mixed with authority, toward me. I represented the ideal young girl for him: pure, innocent, irreproachable, and fragile. He appointed himself my attentive servant, my support, my guide. The other side of this flattering state of affairs was the instant revocation of my freedom. From then on, Sigmund would have a very firm say about any show of feelings aimed at me by anyone. Extra strict, my new guardian focused on my every move. He needed to know who I was seeing. It was then that I discovered his pathological jealousy. An uncontrollable hate spewed forth from Sigmund one day when a cousin of mine, Max Mayer—engaged to someone else—showed an interest in me. I was forbidden to use my cousin's first name; I must address him only as Mr. Mayer! That struck me as too silly, and I continued calling him Max. The same thing happened with Fritz Wahle, my cousin's fiancé. Fritz had been a dear friend, a brother with whom I always enjoyed talking. He was a musician. Sigmund, wary of artists in general, accused them of having a special power of seduction over women. He hit the ceiling once when he learned that Fritz had kissed me—on the cheek, of course.

His state of fury and his doubts about me were truly frightening. This said, Fritz had declared for all to hear that if Freud made me unhappy, he would, quite simply, kill him! Rather excessive, to be sure. No sense of humor here. Sigmund put a stop to our socializing, which chagrined me enormously.

It was clear that my mother didn't appreciate my new beau. Nothing Sigmund could do or say would change her mind: "He does not come from a proper family." This *Galizianer* didn't fit the bill for her. "He is studying to become a doctor," I insisted, "a researcher with a brilliant future ahead of him!" "An atheist, with no fortune!" was all she would answer. "And besides, doctors are a dime a dozen in Vienna. What is so special about Sigmund?"

I was sent away to my uncle Elias's. It would do me good, my mother declared. I would surely forget Sigmund. Little did she know whom she was dealing with.

There was no way Sigmund would let me forget him. His passionate letters, one after the other, invaded my summer. I was his love, his darling, his princess. My absence had plunged him into despair. His letters were dear, sometimes a little childish, and filled with purple prose, I realize today. *At the appointed day, I will come for you, and we will enjoy a happiness unhindered by any cloud, in perfect intimacy.* Or, *When the world sees you have become my dear wife and bear my name, we shall share happy and calm days until the time when eternal sleep comes and closes our eyes.* In one of his letters, Sigmund described in detail the future furnishings of our "sweet home," our linen, our clothes. A bit childish, as I read it today. For a young woman to harbor such romantic dreams, in those days, I understand. But Sigmund!

During all this exchange of letters, Sigmund was tightening his grip on his role of mentor or father. When one day he sent me a gift I considered far too expensive, I thanked him, adding my concern about the extravagance. Sigmund's reply came fast and furious, using the third person: "Martha must cease admonishing so categorically: 'You mustn't do this!' She is no longer the eldest daughter, or the superior sister. From now on, she is young, engaged now for a week, and will cease being caustic once and for all." Here I had been under the impression that once I was engaged, I would join the adult world, assume the status of a woman! For Sigmund it was the opposite. Under his protection and authority, I was to return to an earlier stage of my life—to my youth, or even childhood. Of the day he first saw me—"the day that changed his life," as Sigmund wrote later—he referred to that "little girl chatting with my sisters in such a charming way, as she was peeling her apple." I fit well in his family tableau, with his virgin sisters—all of whom he dominated. I realized then how important his image of me as young girl was. In *The Sorrows of Young Werther*, a book I had not yet read but one Sigmund talked about, Werther discovers Charlotte in a similar idyllic tableau, and falls in love with her—a virgin lovingly peeling an apple for the other virgins who surround her.

His propensity for collecting adoring women around him continued; after me there was Minna, and later on others—all of us playing the role his sisters and mother had before us.

Sigmund's demands flattered me. Whether or not they also troubled me, I did nothing to change our roles. Sigmund's passion had a sure way of making me melt. Furthermore, how could I doubt a man of his caliber who constantly assured me of our future happiness?

Aren't all beginnings of romance wonderful? I have difficulty recognizing the young, naive girl I then was.

Everything Sigmund asked of me, even the most preposterous request, was carried out with utter delight. Was it love? Indeed it was! Discovering passion for the first time in my life had transformed me. It helped me gain new self-confidence. For someone whose shyness had paralyzed her every move socially until now, Sigmund's passion empowered me. Feeling loved, wanted, transformed me. A new persona emerged. The notion that my presence, or absence, could alter this important man's happiness gave me an extraordinary sensation of strength. I, like all those before me, abandoned myself into that helpless love mode—with gratitude. For me, it was a magical time.

Sigmund, at the rate of a new letter every day, did everything to keep me floating in this beatitude. My not replying immediately provoked avalanches of complaints and re-proaches. I also was learning the degree to which Sigmund was jealous—of everyone, it seemed. My brother Eli, to whom I was close, became one of his early targets. Inventing reason after reason to criticize Eli, Sigmund tried downgrading him in my eyes, hoping for a rupture of sorts between us—to no avail. Finally, Sigmund did succeed: because of some obscure money problems I never understood, he obliged me to stop seeing my brother for years!

That character trait in Sigmund began to upset me greatly. What kind of husband was he going to be if, barely engaged, he already displayed such authority, demanding exclusivity, in effect robbing me of any kind of freedom? The other side of this upsetting behavior, of course, was something I couldn't help but find irresistible: his passion. It was precisely that passion that engendered his possessive attitude, I kept telling myself, an attitude that, I must confess, also flattered me no end. Experiencing for the first time what it meant to be precious to another person—irreplaceable, in fact—had a way of sending me into paroxysms of joy. I would do nothing to lose the place in a man's heart I had dreamed of for so long.

As the years passed, I have come to question how being engaged to me could have triggered such storms in Sigmund. How could the shy, unassuming, not ever very pretty young girl I was have stolen the heart of a man like Sigmund Freud? Mystery plays a large, intangible part in any human encounter, I know, but still, our improbable match remains a mystery to me to this day.

Search as I may, I can't find any reason for his choice.

Certainly nothing that could justify the unbounded passion he clearly felt for me. Sigmund knew my brother long before meeting me, and was therefore aware of my origins when he met me: a proper young lady from a good middle-class Hamburg family—not an unimportant factor for Sigmund, I later learned. As for Sigmund, his own mother represented all the Galician Jew's characteristics—my mother's vociferations had been right, after all. He had tried as best he could to shed his roots, dearly hoping to be perceived as a real German. A secular Jew, he didn't appear different from other middle-class men in this country. Sigmund's classic education in the Leopoldstadt Gymnasium had contributed greatly to his desire to be fully integrated. A woman who shared his views was what he was looking for. He hadn't yet made a clean enough break from his family to allow himself to look for a Gentile mate. Did a German Jew strike him as an ideal compromise? Forgetting the fact that, unlike Sigmund, I was a practicing Jew—and it took a great deal of effort on his part to undo my practicing side—I probably seemed to him in many ways the perfect model of a potential wife. For one thing, I stood at the opposite end of the pole from his mother. If she was nervous, excitable, seductive, and imperious, I was a model of calmness, neatness, and submissiveness. It was clear from the start that Sigmund appreciated and welcomed these attributes, and I had no trouble conforming to his ideal woman. Sigmund made no bones about letting me know that "in the truest sense of the term, I was not a beauty, at least in the strict painterly sense." His love for truth sometimes made him cruel. If I did not take umbrage then, it was because, by way of reparation, he quickly recited the list of all the other qualities in me that he so appreciated, which he insisted represented what all men craved in their wives: generosity, wisdom, and tenderness. Sigmund's "reassuring words" only managed to throw me into an uneasy state.

In that, I also differed from his mother. Everyone sang her praise, declaring her one of the most beautiful women of her day. Until late into her nineties, she continued to be seductive. Strange how, at the start of our relationship, Sigmund hoped, and actually formulated the wish, that I play the role of mother for him, one who would protect him from the ills of the world, from solitude, and whose love would place him far above everyone else. I was to be pure, wise, with a perfect balance of strength and sweetness, and renounce the temptations of the outside world. This, he continued, would enable him to fulfill his dreams of creating and exploring unknown territories. How could he have seen in me—that innocent and ignorant girl, sitting with his sisters peeling an apple—the woman who would guarantee him all that security? It still puzzled me. Was it my serious expression? my calm nature? perhaps even my retiring personality, that misled him into thinking I was strong?

Another thought came to me. His mother adored Sigmund. As for Sigi, he remained deeply attached to her, however discreetly. Upon reading *Interpretation of Dreams*, I understood that his discretion did in fact mask his passion for his mother. I often thought that someone like myself, in every way different from his mother, was what he needed. My personality—or lack thereof—would, in his mind, in no way crowd the place his mother held. No one could ever accuse Sigmund of finding a wife resembling his mother, unless the disguise was too obvious, too perfect.

The first eighteen months of our engagement resembled a roller-coaster, full of wild ups and downs. Sigi's constant declarations of love, his demands, his jealousy wore me out. It reached its peak when Sigmund started reproaching me for my attachment to my mother, accusing me of being far too submissive to her. He couldn't countenance the competition, I suppose. He also no doubt felt my mother's serious reservations about him. "She will always remain a stranger," Sigmund wrote me one day. "Her pleasant manner is lined with condescension. Furthermore, her need to be admired drives me mad. I foresee that much of what I do will displease her, and I have no intention of modifying my behavior."

This said, Sigmund's distaste for her never succeeded in making me break with my mother. This was probably the only point in our marriage about which I managed to resist him.

As I wandered to the window to stare out at the night, as I often do, I tried capturing nature's many subtle noises, those I can perceive more clearly at night—the whistling of the wind in the trees, the grating doors of our gate, the whisper of light rain or, at other times, when it comes down hard, banging against the window. "How will it all end up when I no longer hear this nocturnal music, once I close my eyes for good?" How absurd, I realized. In this final sleep, no dream or any sort of sound will come to interrupt it. "And how will it feel not to wake up, this last time?" Again, while I chased this ridiculous thought, another nagging one became louder: "After this life, what *is* out there?"

9

Maresfield Gardens
November 30, 1946

Dear Mary,

The multitude of visits these past few days has made it impossible for me to sit down and reply to your last letter.

Being once again forced to play the part of the grieving widow, I am painfully aware that it was never me people were concerned about, which irritated me no end. I must say, these visits, with their endless displays of admiration, demonstrations of devotion for the great man, are beginning to get on my nerves. Your caring, your probing into my life, have doubtless spoiled me. After all these years, I may well have become vain after all.

I enjoyed your latest letter. As always. Your infinite discretion about yourself made me worry that you may actually be feeling lonely, perhaps even unhappy. I had been concerned about you. Thank you for reassuring me. Might your lifestyle appear scandalous to me? you ask. Forty or fifty years ago, I would have condemned it as such, yes. Do remember that in those days, in my milieu and the particularly pious family I came from, living with a man without being married was unthinkable for a virtuous lady. Today, how I envy your freedom, and how I regret not having known any myself!

What did I perceive of Sigmund's work during our early married years? you ask. Very little, or nothing. As I mentioned, the moment we were married, Sigmund stopped sharing this important part of his life. Well before our marriage, he had made it clear that the management of our home was to be my basic, if not sole, preoccupation. It was only when I read his books years later that I entered and understood Sigmund's universe.

What became clear to me, however, during those early days of our marriage, was how tormented his research seemed to make him. Starting in 1896, Sigmund became increasingly somber. On December 3, Anna's first birthday, his father died after a long illness, plunging Sigmund into absolute despair. It surprised me, since I had never noticed any particularly strong attachment on his part to his father. Sigmund's grief put a temporary halt to his work. From that moment on, he became secretive. Isolating himself in his study, behind closed doors, he would spend hours writing to Wilhelm. Only much later did I realize upon reading his *Interpretation of Dreams* that, fully conscious of how abnormal his grief was, he was examining it from a scientific viewpoint. The entanglement of autobiography and science left the psychiatric community perplexed. Sigmund decided to undergo self-analysis. This process was, as expected, not without its consequences. At the time, unaware of the reason behind them, I saw with a growing concern a number of strange symptoms. Sigmund would be sick one day; a few days later he would complain of heart problems, all of which made him turn to Wilhelm for help. Only Wilhelm was capable of curing him, Sigmund declared. Minna and I were silent and helpless observers of his despair, as well as of his bouts of euphoria.

Although Sigmund would often wake up with nightmares in a cold sweat, he never elaborated on any of them to us. What had happened to the strong man, my protector, who always found a reassuring solution to my problems? He had changed so drastically. There apparently was another reason for his many anxieties. In 1897, an essential part of his theory—that all neuroses could be explained by some sexual trauma suffered in childhood—had collapsed. After long studies, and through his own medical experience—personal and other—he came to the conclusion that this was pure fantasy on his part. The evolution of his theory had everything to do with his discovering the Oedipus complex. It painfully led Sigmund to understand that the profound grief his father's death had brought him was nothing but the guilt of an early death wish, one that would have elevated him to his mother's sole lover.

If I had had any notion of this at the time, I know I would have dismissed it as extravagant and in terrible taste. Like most of my contemporaries, I refused to accept the presence of erotic feelings in children, including mine, who, I was certain, were pure, innocent, and devoid of any such base feelings. Interestingly, because Sigmund never made any mention of his research or discoveries within the family, our children were being raised like those of all our friends, in a nice middle-class manner, with the same prudish, old-fashioned credos prevailing.

In 1897 a book Wilhelm Fliess published entitled *The Biological Relationship between the Nose and Female Genital Organs* gave us, as might be expected, much concern. Minna and I decided to take the book from Sigi's study and read it. Its arcane gibberish, so far from Sigmund's limpid prose, made me close the volume. Minna pursued it to the end, and proceeded to translate it for me, as best she could. Our initial reaction was to burst into giggles. Contrary to Sigmund's theories—although Wilhelm attributed many nervous troubles to sexuality as well—he claimed that the nasal mucus and the feminine genital organs were closely related. According to him, this analogy permitted the cure of sexual problems by some nasal intervention. On the other hand, Wilhelm believed he had discovered some fundamental law in vital activities, a kind of periodicity of twenty-three or twenty-eight days, depending on the sexes, that he was obsessively trying to find with the help of some obscure calculations. "The man is certifiably crazy!" Minna concluded.

I wondered whether, in the middle of Wilhelm's crazy theories, there wasn't something valid. I also wondered whether my husband himself wasn't becoming crazy. This new numerology had gotten to Sigmund. He found it important and wonderful. In retrospect, I think he was looking for some infallible concept based on the feminine cycle. Not so far-fetched, if one remembered Dr. Ogino, who did develop this notion with some success. What I do recall is thinking that if indeed Wilhelm had discovered some brilliant theory, I was also convinced he was at the same time suffering from a serious form of insanity. All these theoretical discoveries must have affected to some degree Sigmund's sensitivity. Numbers played a definite role for him, as did superstition. Following some convoluted calculation Sigmund became convinced he would die at age sixty-one, and that time was therefore of the essence if he was to make a discovery that would leave his name to posterity. When our daughter Mathilde became quite ill—we were concerned she wouldn't make it—to my consternation, Sigmund fetched one of his favorite statuettes and threw it on the floor! An offering to assuage the god's fury?

How could anyone be both atheist and superstitious? I asked myself. Was Sigmund really the atheist he claimed to be?

Meanwhile, Wilhelm was becoming dangerous. A young lady, Emma Eckstein, an acquaintance of ours and a patient of Sigmund's, found herself in serious danger after having been referred to Wilhelm with some kind of sexual disorder. He operated on her nose; she became terribly ill, and serious complications followed. At death's door, she was rescued by a Viennese specialist, who discovered that Wilhelm had left some gauze, saturated with iodine, inside her wound! This frightening episode left Sigmund immensely tormented. How could he have placed his trust in this man? While he continued calling Wilhelm his magician, he harbored resentment and guilt. It had occurred to me at the time that one of the reasons Sigmund had stopped his analysis of Emma, and referred her to Wilhelm, was his concern about her charm. Could her sexual issues have had something to do with Sigmund? If indeed they had, Sigmund did not behave any better than his friend Dr. Breuer had with young Bertha. And what about Wilhelm's incredible negligence? An *acte manqué*, to use Sigmund's terminology—an aggressive act of retaliation against Sigmund? Although it took years for Sigmund to loosen his bonds with Wilhelm, this deplorable incident did have its repercussions, making serious difficulties for their friendship.

Sigmund had always been vulnerable to sudden enthusiasms. This time, the odd choice was cocaine. He was convinced he had made the discovery of the century. This happened during the long period of our engagement. Professor

Meynert, with whom Sigmund had worked, introduced the drug to him. Sigmund was convinced cocaine was a cure-all, which worried me greatly. Cocaine, he kept insisting, would take care of cardiac troubles, as well as general fatigue. When he decided to try it on himself, I became seriously concerned. It was simply marvelous! he insisted. He was in a permanent state of euphoria; there were no limits to his work capacity! He no longer needed to feed himself. All Sigmund's gastric problems had vanished, thanks to the drug. He went on to write about the drug's healing properties, assuring the reader that one need have no concern about addiction.

Being utterly ignorant on the subject, I had no way of knowing whether he was right or wrong. Nonetheless, Sigmund frightened me. I soon saw that my concerns were justified. He had thrown himself into the tunnel of his passion, claiming it took care of all quotidian ills. Completely addicted, he was ignoring its dangers. But in his ecstasy, he had neglected cocaine's anesthetic properties. Dr. Koller, an ophthalmologic surgeon friend of his to whom Sigmund confided, grasping its medicinal potential, tried it—with great glory and success. As for Sigmund, he received only flack, being castigated for having touted the drug's virtues. Thankfully, no one knew he himself had become addicted.

Thinking back, I question how Sigmund could have behaved so imprudently. During this period, he even went so far as to suggest I try a weak dose of cocaine. "It will cure all the various ills you complain about!" he assured me. As someone who never took any medication, I submitted to his will and, with apprehension, obeyed. Once or twice I dutifully took what Sigmund prepared for me. What he never knew, however, was that the drug soon found its way into my wastebasket. And, of course, my guilt over disobeying him, and wasting such an expensive drug, haunted me for a long while. If he had been told the truth, I know he would never have forgiven me.

As the old century was inching toward the new, Sigmund and Wilhelm's close bonds loosened even further, and they were finally severed. In 1903, Minna and I breathed a collective sigh of relief: the two parted ways, for some obscure reason having to do with plagiarism! The reason for this important split mattered little to Minna and me. Privately, the two of us celebrated the rupture. Sigmund got more and more absorbed in his work, and his friend slowly vanished into some distant past. We both noticed that Sigmund's mood improved radically. He became more relaxed. However, when his *Interpretation of Dreams,* published in 1900, did not become the triumph he had expected, Sigmund was stung. The same held for his *Studies in Hysteria,* which suffered the same fate. The medical community was definitely thumbing its nose at Sigmund's work, going so far as to dub him a charlatan. When later his *Psychopathology of Everyday Life* came out, and was hardly noticed, Sigmund hit a new low. Feeling hopelessly misunderstood, he turned with even more vigor to his solitary research and writing.

Meanwhile, we were still waiting for the steady flow of faithful patients that would provide us with some financial security. The number of his patients seemed to fluctuate between two and ten, and as the century waned, our situation became downright catastrophic. How would we be able to take care of our children? The Viennese medical community had rejected Sigmund as a "truant of a Jew whose only focus was sexuality." It became clear that counting on referrals from colleagues had become a dream. In 1897, as Sigmund was invited only now and then to lecture around the country, he saw the urgent need to apply for a visiting professorship, a purely honorific title that didn't oblige him to teach. But we all knew that that distinction would mean a great deal to the Viennese public, which was known for being impressed by titles. Being called Herr Professor was indeed far more enviable than merely Herr Doctor! By 1901 Sigmund decided to take things into his own hands, and actively appealed to everyone he knew for personal recommendations. As expected, none of his professors came through. A patient of his, Baroness von Ferstel, made it her mission. Running into a minister at one of her social functions, she talked at great length about Sigmund, extracting from the dignitary the promise that he would help out. Not satisfied with this promise, the baroness went so far as to donate one of her own valuable paintings to the minister—which he gladly accepted for his collection. That seemed to do it. Sigmund's professorship was granted. As I look at my husband's prestigious title—ever so deserved—I am sadly reminded of its dubious origin.

Before long, just as we had hoped, there was an immediate correlation between Sigmund's new title and an influx of patients, and our financial problems lessened. My own life also improved to some degree, with the help my sister was providing. I felt less lonely in my daily tasks, and overseeing the tricky routine of my home became easier.

Minna and I meanwhile acknowledged an important

turning point in our respective lives: we were both over forty. Looking in the mirror, I could see the irreversible marks time had carved on my face and figure. Although each day I made a point of concealing the passage of time by presenting myself cleverly and paying special attention to my wardrobe, I had to come to the conclusion that these efforts were for naught. As for Minna, it had been a long time since she had paid any attention to her physical appearance. She had grown fat, and most of the time she was rather unkempt. Looking recently at a photograph, I see two rather stiff and dry ladies, each looking more austere than the other, as if to confirm they had capitulated to their self-imposed middle-age status.

None of this self-awareness of our age prevented us however from carrying on in the same way we had as young girls, with energy and good spirits. Minna oversaw the domestic routine and the children's homework, and I took care of Sigmund in every detail—from his clothes to the general schedule—organizing food supplies, instructing the cook on each menu, and making sure lunch was served at one o'clock sharp each day. Lunch consisted mainly of the Viennese specialty called *Tafelspitz*—boiled beef and vegetables, with a horseradish sauce—which Sigmund loved. Meanwhile, as Minna, acting as Sigmund's unofficial secretary, was happily spending endless hours next to him, I had ceased being jealous. Through her, I would get news of Sigmund's work progress, and that was fine with me.

I missed my mother, who I invited year in and year out to come and visit, and who constantly refused my invitations. When she finally did come, it was only for a brief visit. She had never taken to Vienna, calling it a city of crass profit and debauchery. In fact, Sodom and Gomorrah was her term! While earlier on the tension between Sigmund and my mother had been palpable, they both had now come to some kind of tacit understanding and behaved in a civilized manner toward each other. The brevity of her stays, it turned out, had to do with our impiety. Not only did she object to my having turned my back on our religion, but the fact that our children were being raised without the slightest rudiment of their ancestors' religion was intolerable to her.

Also, she never felt comfortable with our eating habits. We were not following ancient rabbinical food proscriptions, and that was simply unacceptable. Nevertheless, from the time of her first visit, I had dutifully purchased a special set of china and silverware, to be used only by her. Under no circumstance, I instructed the domestics, were they to mix these sets with our own. This special set of china just for her would make it acceptable for her to eat without fear while visiting us. There would be no blasphemy, and she would not be contaminated by any unkosher food. Each time we walked past the butcher shop, she quickly turned her head the other way in disgust. And of course, she refused all meat. As for the rest of our offerings, namely dairy and fish, her suspicion prevailed. She ended up eating only boiled vegetables and bread.

Most of her time was spent sitting by the window, reading her prayer book. Seeing her lips move silently each time I passed through the room touched me, making me want to hug her. I was watching my mother age, right before my eyes. The children were slightly intimidated by her aloof attitude. Unlike Sigmund's mother, who, with a big scream of joy always greeted them with open arms, my mother's style was distant. "Why is Grandma Emmeline always muttering to herself while reading her big book?" they would ask. "And we don't understand the gestures she makes when she reads, either. . . ."

I couldn't answer properly, always embarrassed and concerned they would ask why we didn't do that as well. I wasn't ready to tell them that their father had outlawed all religion in our house. It was difficult to explain, at their young age, that they too had been forbidden any religious instruction. I didn't feel it necessary for them to be privy to our marital disagreements on the subject. Later, as adolescents, they viewed archaic religious practices with a certain amusement. Adopting their father's position seemed the natural thing to do. Minna, for her part, while condemning our lay education, was not as vehement as my mother; she could never bring herself to formulate any reproach to Sigi, at least to his face. With much rigor, and despite living with us pagans, she had somehow managed to remain faithful to our family traditions. Fasting at Yom Kippur, she never touched pork—something Sigmund liked. In fact, he had no food restrictions. In marrying Sigmund, I had decided once and for all not to oppose his ideas, and I did renounce all religious practices. I recall trying to light the candles on the Sabbath, only to have my wrist slapped by Sigmund. From then on, I knew enough never to light candles on Sabbath again. But it didn't prevent my suffering a lingering guilt.

In 1910 my mother died. It left me bereft. The unarticulated complicity between us, which had been such comfort to me those last several years, was now gone forever.

Sigmund's imperious need for order caused our life to be arranged with utter precision, regulated like a sheet of music.

After lunch, Sigmund would go for a walk through the city for a good hour. With an almost Germanic sense of hygiene, of which I approved, he strongly believed in daily exercise. In the course of his walks, Sigmund would buy his stock of cigars. He smoked roughly a pack a day. We later learned that that was one of the worst things he could ever have done. But he simply could not imagine life, and his work in particular, without smoking. Our whole house smelled of tobacco, especially his office. I often wondered how his patients could tolerate that smell for an entire hour. For us family, it was part and parcel of our life, as was Sigmund's beard, or the way he looked at you. None of us ever dared make a remark to him about it. He only stopped smoking at the urging of his friend Wilhelm when he was thought to have developed a heart problem. But that lasted only a short while. For Sigmund, smoking was a veritable drug.

As soon as Sigmund returned to his office after lunch, Minna and I would go out for our walk, weather permitting. Or we would immerse ourselves in some manual work in the living room. It was as if we had gone back to our early days in Wandsbeck, when we both would sit under our linden tree, busily preparing our respective trousseaus. There was a great deal of delicate embroidering of tablecloths, hemming of thick linen kitchen towels and heavy percale sheets. As often when women work together on some project, we always spoke in whispers.

In the evening, the youngest of our children ate before we did and were promptly ushered to bed before we sat down for our own supper. Lost in his thoughts, Sigmund often remained silent at the table while Minna, the older children, and I carried on a conversation. And more often than not, after dinner Sigmund would retire to his office, often working late into the night.

Another of our unshakable habits had to do with Sigmund's family. In our early married days, we used to have regular Sunday lunches at the Freuds' on Kaiser-Josefstrasse, giving me a chance to visit with his sisters, something I always enjoyed. After Sigmund's father died, Sigmund made it a ritual to pay a visit to his mother on Sunday morning, with a bouquet of flowers, accompanied by one or several children. Each Sunday evening she would come to our home for dinner, with Dolfi, who never left her mother for a moment. Poor dear, all her sisters had married and flown the coop. The unwritten rule in families in those days dictated that the remaining unmarried child be the care-giver to the widowed mother—a job no one envied.

I will now confess to you, Mary, something I have never told anyone else: I hated my mother-in-law. In that respect, Minna's presence was of great help to me in these Sunday visits. She wasn't intimidated by this tyrannical and temperamental woman, who could not tolerate not being the center of attention. We all had to hang on her every word, her every wish. Furthermore, I couldn't stand watching how terribly she treated Dolfi. Even worse was Sigmund's total awe of, and submission to, her. Oblivious of her many negative sides, he was an adoring son. With unflinching composure, I made sure never to reveal my true feelings to Sigmund. The only one to whom I could vent my anger, decompress, and speak openly, was Minna, which was a great relief to me. She of course chimed in with her own recriminations, which gave her pleasure as well. And we inevitably ended up having a good laugh about it.

My mother-in-law lived with undiminished energy to the ripe old age of ninety-five, as demanding as ever. As far as Dolfi was concerned, she continued making scenes about unimportant things, such as refusing to wear a certain hat. Sigmund's attachment to his mother never ceased to intrigue me. It had always been clear that she preferred Sigmund to her other children. Whenever he appeared, she would literally throw herself into his arms, smothering him with declarations of love, all of which I found in very poor taste. Sigmund, overwhelmed by her exaggerated display of emotion, maintained an attitude that could best be described as cold, defensive. Always keeping his sense of filial duty, however, he demonstrated great respect for his mother. The Sunday visits with flowers went on like clockwork, followed by his mother's visits for supper at our house. After supper, gallantly taking her arm, Sigmund would accompany her each Sunday evening back home. Beneath his distant demeanor, I detected complex feelings.

Sigmund has written about his love for his young mother, and how puzzled he was by his parents' age difference. As a young child, Sigmund had trouble reconciling himself with the fact that they were married. Later, the thought of dying before his mother—the image of her pain upon his disappearance—terrified Sigmund, especially after he learned he had cancer. I don't know why, but each time Sigmund expressed these feelings to me, I felt terribly uneasy. It puzzled me that when he talked about his death, the only grieving person he managed to evoke, and be concerned about, was his mother. What about his wife? His children? Wasn't this link, still so strong at this moment of his life, rather surprising? Today I see the unresolved bond, the knots that had him all tied up. When his mother died, Sigmund was seventy-four years old and terribly ill. Attending her funeral was quite out of the question. I remember his expressing once again his relief at having spared her the grief his death would have caused her. His mother's love must have given Sigmund strength. To the very end, he held fast to the notion that he had been his mother's favorite.

Having put pen to paper to confide in you such intimate and never before disclosed personal thoughts astonishes me greatly. And shocks me. I must once again ask you to promise that, after reading it, you will destroy this letter. The notion that my indiscretions might be seen by others mortifies me.

Dear Mary, I must leave you now until your next letter, which I look forward to reading.

Martha

10

For the past week, anxiety attacks have interrupted my sleep, night after night. I wake up choking, with the terrible feeling of being alone in the world. As I turn my bedside lamp on and look around, I am quickly reassured. My room is there just as before; everything is in place. I force myself out of bed, open my window, and breathe the fresh air deeply: everything outside seems in place as well. The world has not disappeared. My next move is to put on my robe and sit at the table, where my puzzle welcomes me. A few feet away, Anna is sound asleep. It would not occur to me to wake her. True, there is always Paula, who I know would rush to make me a cup of chamomile tea, but I refrain from waking her as well.

Could Mary's last letter have provoked this? Inadvertently, of course. She sings the praise of her companion, David. Describing how handsome, intelligent, and tender his manners are, she rhapsodizes about what she feels when David takes her into his arms. Her next phrase is, "For the first time, I am learning what it is to love and be loved. In his arms, I am the happiest woman." Having become very fond of Mary, I am delighted for her. Still, it leads me to reflect on the fact that it has been decades since I was in someone's arms. What's more, the absence of tenderness that only a mother or a lover can give has turned my being into something dry, empty, and abandoned. No one will ever reach for me with open arms; that, I know. Is that what troubles my sleep and shakes me awake?

Dark images haunt me these days. My house is so empty, uninhabited, and frightening. Sigi's face, as it looked during the last months of his life, keeps appearing to me over and over. I picture us arriving in London—two old, fragile people, bewildered and utterly weary from their journey— and then the unexpected enthusiasm of a whole horde of people greeting us. His face had shrunk, his mouth reduced to a line of suffering. I see him again, stretched out in a chaise longue in our garden, not uttering a word, looking past us all. A surge of love came over me again, I remember, but all I could do was express faint gestures of affection, smile, or gently tap his shoulder. An invisible wall was being erected, separating us. "Please, do not upset him," Anna implored, suggesting I leave Sigmund alone and get some rest myself. "Don't worry," she said, "I'll take care of everything!" And indeed, until Sigmund's death, Anna did handle every detail of her father's life and work.

It had long been agreed between Dr. Schur and Sigmund that at the appropriate moment, on Sigmund's signal, Dr. Schur would help Sigmund exit this world with dignity. For a long time Sigmund fought, and with enormous courage. But one day he did call Dr. Schur. That moment had arrived. Dr. Schur turned to Anna—not to me—for her approval. Sobbing, she began saying, "No." She couldn't bear to see her father die. Did she prefer to see him suffer? He who in the last days had become "her thing"? After a long emotional discussion with Dr. Schur, she resigned herself to the inevitable.

As I look back on the way Sigmund's ultimate drama unfolded, I remember thinking: Anna has even managed to rob me of my husband's death.

It was the summer of 1939. For the past few weeks, rampant rumors had been circulating. "Is war really about to start?" everyone was asking. We, of course, avoided the subject in Sigi's presence. Several times a day I would run down to the kitchen to listen to the radio, while Paula and I stared at each other in disbelief. On September 1, we heard loud sirens. Paula burst into the room and whispered close to my ear, "He invaded Poland. War has been declared." "He" being the devil incarnate, the monster that had poisoned our lives and spirits. Three weeks later, Sigi decided to disappear.

For the past week, that image has kept coming clearly back every night. Usually I manage to fall asleep as soon as my head hits the pillow. More often than not, in fact, I fall asleep head down on my unfinished puzzle. But these days, I wait impatiently for the dimness to transform itself into daylight. Daytime is so much easier. I take my time getting dressed, chat with Paula, and do various things around the house. Since Sigi's death, I have been reading a great deal. Not that I couldn't have before, but my education didn't allow me to indulge myself in the face of all that needed to be accomplished. It goes back to our mother, who strictly forbade us to read during the day—a time devoted only to work. Sigmund didn't interfere with my day-to-day routine—he might even have encouraged my reading—but my self-imposed rule prevailed. While he was alive, I never picked up a book.

We are well into December. It is cold, and the sky announces imminent snow. Paula, I am certain, will want to get a tree for our living room, which she'll decorate. Why should I deny her that joy? And besides, we always celebrated Christmas. It was simply one more family party. I remember hearing my mother's voice, long after she died, deep within me, shouting: "What in the world do you think you are doing, celebrating this goy holiday? Are you doing the same with the birth of the false Messiah?" I was never able to bring myself to explain to her that all we wanted to do was live like all the other Viennese. Did we ever? I wonder.

11

Maresfield Gardens
December 16, 1946

Dear Mary,

First, I must thank you for the magnificent package you sent
me. Everything in it—the eggs, the chocolate, the cookies,
the nylon stockings—is still extremely rationed or unfind-
able. Paula, who doesn't know who you are, sends thanks as
well. She can't wait to bake real cakes with real ingredients
now. I gave her the stockings—neither Minna nor I have
ever worn any. She is thrilled.

How did I react when my husband became famous?
you ask. Memory plays tricks these days, stretching and turning time like a rubber band. Why is it that unimportant details seem to stick, while significant ones vanish? The first
fourteen years of my marriage seem to have been very rich in
all sorts of ways. I remember being conscious of it, and wishing it would never stop. The following fourteen years, leading up to the war, are engraved in my memory like a desert
with only a few dots of minor happenings. All the more
strange because this was when Sigmund's glory years were
fast approaching. In 1900, at the time of *Interpretation of
Dreams*, he was still unpopular among the Viennese medical
community, and virtually unknown outside Austria. Fourteen

years later his name had reached America, and he was soon surrounded by admiring disciples. Congresses, conferences, associations focusing on him and his groundbreaking work, were being held all over the world. I never understood what triggered this sudden transformation. It seemed a miracle to us both. All these years of silent research, so often discouraged! All it took were a few key people to begin talking about him, their word spreading like fire, faster and faster, farther and farther. From that moment on, Sigi's success permeated our lives. At home, we reaped its benefits. With glory came new material comfort. Even more appreciated was Sigmund's seemingly much better mood.

While Sigi's existence was widening, mine, on the other hand, was shrinking. Serving as a kind of anchor when he ventured into unknown territory had made me feel indispensable and fulfilled. I represented the discreet and faithful companion, always there, ready to raise his morale. Had I not been—peripherally, of course—part of the edifice he had constructed, and part therefore of his achievements? I remember feeling proud, albeit vicariously. What I could not anticipate, however, was that once he achieved success and recognition, Sigmund would no longer need the anchor I represented, a realization that left me sad.

"My son is Professor Freud!" his mother boasted pompously to whoever would listen. Wasn't she ridiculous to be parading her son's glory? I remember thinking. But . . . wasn't I guilty of the same thing? To be a famous man's wife . . . didn't many envy this prestigious position? But was it really that wonderful for me?

Time was passing. My children had grown, and they too needed me less and less. When Sigmund turned fifty, things became suddenly clear. The children, then between ten and eighteen, were all involved in their respective occupations. The boys' only point of reference was their father, who was becoming more famous with each passing day. As for Mathilde, all she thought about was getting married. Sophie was lost in her adolescent dreams, and Anna, deeply immersed in her studies, had long ago turned her back on me. The role of mother I had been playing up to now was reduced to a mere presence; I was like one of those lovely butterflies pinned on the wall. Sigmund, so conservative and not one to encourage change, needed his butterfly pinned precisely to the same spot.

From 1902 on, several Viennese doctors joined Sigmund regularly, hoping to become initiated into the science Sigmund had so recently coined, which pleased him no end. These doctors would meet each Wednesday evening in Sigmund's waiting room, next to his office. Each morning, after those meetings, I could hear the cleaning lady's horrified sounds as she entered the room filled with cigarette butts, the smell of smoke still hanging heavy in the air. "It's a wonder they didn't all die asphyxiated!" she would shout in horror. Fascinated by these young men and their new ideas, Minna pined to be invited to their sessions. But Sigmund made no move to ask her. Slowly, Minna came to realize that the spot she had been sure was hers and hers alone had been passed on to others. New interlocutors had supplanted her, had invaded her scene. A whole new group of motivated students, all hoping to get a crack at the professor's secrets, was now surrounding him. In those young doctors Sigmund saw not merely new partners but acolytes who could help his spread his ideas in an increasingly wider circle. I saw Sigmund well ensconced in his role of master, addressing his own school. Fully confident in his new theories, he had little room for other ideas from his students.

Gone forever were his days of self-doubt. Sigmund had found what he had been looking for, and the time had come for him to teach it. Isn't self-assurance part of what constitutes genius?

Through word of mouth, Sigmund's name began to spread, first throughout Vienna and Austria, then to the rest of the world. Minna remained Sigmund's traveling companion for a little while longer. He even found time to play a card game or two with her, but the kind of intellectual exchanges they had enjoyed earlier were now history. As far as traveling with the master, it was not long before she had to give up her place to new companions. Time! That unforgiving time that ages women mercilessly, while transforming men into powerful and seductive beings!

By 1907, Sigmund had attained celebrity status. Money was no longer an issue for us. In fact, Sigmund could not accommodate all the demands on his time anymore: his reputation had gone beyond our borders and was such that foreign patients were arriving in droves to be analyzed on Berggasse. Sigmund was especially pleased that many were returning home, introducing psychoanalysis in their own countries. Some stayed longer and became his most faithful friends. Karl Abraham, for one, a Berliner I liked particularly—I had even entertained the idea of his becoming interested in our daughters—Sandor Ferenczi, for another, the Hungarian with bulging eyes and glasses; Ernst Jones, the Englishman with a round head and eyes like buttonholes;

and the young Otto Rank, who, not being a doctor, ended up working as Sigmund's secretary. Today, the only one still with us is Dr. Jones, as you know.

That same year, 1907, Sigmund met someone with whom he became as infatuated as he had been with Wilhelm. This time it was a young clinical and experimental psychiatrist from Zurich. In March of that year, we saw a tall, dashing young man—around thirty—sporting a pleasant face with a thin mustache arrive at Bergstrasse. His serious expression and stiff attitude brought back some adolescent dreams of mine. The two men would meet early in the morning, disappear behind closed doors, and work late into the night—often emerging thirteen hours later. The two would continue their intense discussions over dinner, their eyes locked, without paying the slightest heed to Minna or me. Needless to say, Minna, as usual, had trouble hiding her irritation. And as for me, I was looking with fascination at this man, a good twenty years younger than my husband and animated by the same passion as Sigmund. How I envied them! Their lives were decidedly so interesting, whereas mine . . .

Sigmund would join us after his guest had left, inhaling his cigar, praising the young man—Carl Gustav Jung—who had entered his life and understood everything! Sigmund was exultant! Jung had read his *Interpretation of Dreams* not once but twice and was busy not only applying Sigmund's method but defending it publicly. "Oh," replied Minna, whose blood had been boiling for a while. "How can he? He is far too goy to really understand!"

Sigmund heard her remark, cast an angry look over at her. "It's you who does not understand a thing, my dear Minna! It is precisely because he is goy that he interests me.

And Swiss. There are dozens of doctors, Viennese Jews, around me. They bring me nothing. Furthermore, were I to stay within that small universe, it wouldn't be long before being accused of reducing psychoanalysis to a Jewish science.

"No, really. What I now need is foreign endorsement. It's imperative for my discovery to be universally recognized. And with a man of such value, I feel confident in the future. Of all people, he is the one to properly proselytize and support my work."

That was that. From now on, Sigmund would closet himself in his study each evening and write to his young colleague. Envelopes bearing Zurich stamps arrived at our house on a regular basis. "How could Sigmund fall once again as he did with Wilhelm?" Minna implored. "How could he let himself be seduced by those childish exchanges? It will end badly! Mark my words!"

In 1907, after long conflicts that had begun at the end of the 1890s, the emperor granted the Austrian nation the universal right to vote. The following year, Sigmund requested his citizenship and received it, but he didn't much use his right to vote. For us women it changed nothing. I guess we did not belong to that new universe. For the past fifteen years, my friend Bertha, an ardent feminist—also traveling throughout Europe saving children, victims of pogroms—was proselytizing for the feminist cause. It had no effect on me. Why were women intent on impinging on men's territories? I kept asking. These women terrified me; their world was utterly alien to me. Anyway, I was convinced they would fail. As it turned out, I was wrong. Feminists battled relentlessly, and ultimately gained some important rights. The education I had received, plus living with a husband of a strongly conservative bent, did not pave the way for me to become a suffragette.

Nearing fifty, I was beginning to experience how fast time seems to go by as one gets older—something my mother had often talked about, but to which I had paid little attention at the time. Now, I discovered, seasons disappeared quickly, one after the other. My children had jumped from adolescence to adulthood in the blink of an eye, while I stood still. The worst was over, I was convinced. From now on we would sail smoothly toward a brilliant future. My husband's career would grow by leaps and bounds, the children would enter adult life on a solid footing, there would be weddings and births. Little did I imagine the difficulties still in store for us.

Meanwhile, to the astonishment of everyone, Sigmund and his young Swiss friend were growing closer and closer. Framed photographs of Jung were now in prominent display on Sigmund's desk. Minna and I watched with fascination as my husband's Viennese students' jealousy reached new heights when Sigmund, so taken with Jung, made noises about adopting him as his spiritual son.

Nothing escaped Minna, who was growing more bitter by the day. Funny how patterns repeat themselves. As had been the case with me during our engagement, and then later with Wilhelm, Sigmund demanded that his new friend answer his letters by return mail. Failing that, Sigmund would pace nervously, smoking his cigar, until a letter arrived. "No mail today!" Minna would gleefully announce at lunch, while Sigmund darted a somber look over at her. Papers were exchanged between the two men on a regular basis. As soon as an article arrived, I saw that Sigmund would immerse himself in it. Sometimes Minna would manage to pilfer a document or two from Sigmund's desk and read it to me. "It makes absolutely no sense!" she would comment acidly.

Aware of her bad faith, I pretended to agree. I knew very well that all she was waiting for was some imminent rupture. "Any relationship that starts with such passion has to crash," she insisted. And indeed small frictions did begin to emerge. Jung, it turned out, wasn't the docile student he had first seemed. He even dared question some of Sigmund's most cherished concepts, infantile sexuality and the Oedipus complex. Making an effort to overcome his irritation, Sigmund carried on, certain of his eventual victory. It was simply impossible for Sigmund to believe that his adoptive son would reject his theory. That same year, the first international psychoanalytical congress, which promised to be of great importance, took place in Salzburg.

In 1909, something extremely odd occurred in Sigmund's office when his pupil had returned to visit. In the course of examining their respective work, Jung asked Sigmund out of the blue what he thought of occultism. "Pure nonsense!" Sigmund predictably answered. At that very moment, apparently out of nowhere, a huge noise was heard in the bookshelves. Both men jumped in their seats.

"You see, this is what is called 'catalytic of exteriorization'!"

"What utter nonsense!" Sigmund retorted. "Rubbish!"

"How wrong you are," said Jung. "And to prove it to you, I predict that the same huge noise will return."

Sure enough, an identical noise indeed followed, coming from the same place. Sigmund emerged from his office deeply perturbed. I couldn't figure out whether it was the event itself that had upset him, or having discovered an obscure and unsuspected side to his protégé.

After Jung left, Sigmund spent the rest of the evening attempting to prove to us that none of what had happened in his office had any meaning, saying, "All superstitions emanate from motives of the subconscious!" His insistence only made me wonder whether he wasn't try to convince himself. Minna kept silent, but I could feel a tremendous satisfaction mounting in her. The expression on her face seemed to say, "You see, the worm is in the apple. What is about to follow is obvious!" When she left to go up to her room, she whispered to me, "Another crazy! Why on earth does Sigmund always manage to fall for this kind of sick fellow?"

Still, the friendship was far from over. That same year, they traveled together to America as guests of Clark University, which was celebrating its twentieth anniversary. Together with Sandor Ferenczi, they boarded a ship in Bremen, where they had rendezvoused. Ferenczi, like so many in Sigmund's entourage at the time, was upset by Sigmund's obvious preference for the Swiss analyst. Ferenczi told me that when in the course of their trip, Jung harped with undue insistence to Sigmund on something that was apparently a practice of the region—a kind of mummification of cadavers in peat—Sigmund turned white and fainted. There was no question, Ferenczi concluded, that Jung was expressing a death wish to Sigmund.

A bit far-fetched, I thought at the time; this undoubtedly reflected Ferenczi's own malevolent feelings toward his rival.

What concerned me upon hearing all this was my husband's health. The three men spent most of the crossing telling one another their dreams and analyzing them, apparently. It didn't seem to have done them much good, I remember thinking. By the time they returned, all three seemed cool to one another. "There was nothing abnormal about Jung asking his master to interpret his dreams," Ferenczi said, "but for Jung to interpret Sigmund's dreams was uncommonly arrogant on his part."

Ferenczi's sole ambition, it was obvious, was to take Jung's place. Persisting in his desire to get close to Sigmund, the following summer Ferenczi arranged to spend a few days near the house we were renting in Berchtesgaden. In 1910 he succeeded in accompanying Sigmund to Sicily—a journey that proved less than satisfactory to him, as Sigmund let it be known how much he missed his Swiss protégé.

My husband's letters from the United States were mainly about his dislike of Americans—their lack of education, the carelessness with which they had received him, and his inability to digest their food. In fact, Sigmund's digestive problems, which never seemed to go away, were nothing new. He had named his stomach "Conrad," and often referred to "Conrad misbehaving." In America, however, "Conrad" gave him more problems than ever before. There was no question, as I mentioned, that despite the warm reception his work received there, and the increasing number of his American patients, Sigmund did not enjoy your country, and never changed his opinion. Why did Sigmund show such a pronounced aversion to America? While I cannot really say for sure, I wonder if my brother Eli, who had immigrated there back in 1892 and been successful, and Sigmund's sister Anna, the only one who had escaped his influence, didn't have something to do with his negative feelings. When Jung, whose theoretical positions were so diametrically opposed to Sigmund's, had the nerve to be welcomed in America with great enthusiasm, it must have been for Sigmund the last straw.

After their return from America, the two men began to put some distance between themselves, and before long things went rapidly downhill. Increasingly secretive about his research, Jung began to limit his visits, which Sigmund found difficult to accept, having imagined that his relationship with Jung would replicate that with Wilhelm. Meanwhile, Jung was quietly pursuing his research in the realm of mythology, keeping his findings from Sigmund—which understandably infuriated him. Nonetheless, overcoming his personal feelings and reservations, Sigmund helped push Jung's nomination as president of the International Association of Psychoanalysis. The new honor bestowed upon Jung by Sigmund did little to alter Jung's attitude. Jung remained aloof, to Sigmund's mounting irritation. "An ingrate! The more I give him, the greater his distance and reserve!" he lamented. The rift became even more pronounced when Sigmund learned that Jung was not fulfilling his directorial obligations at the association.

During the Weimar Congress in 1911, Jung presented his theory and method—entirely different from that of Sigmund—for treating phantasm as it relates to mythology. Sigmund let it go by without reacting until the following year, when Jung published *Symbols of Transformation*, which clearly demonstrated his departure from his master's ideas. By taking a separate road, Jung became Sigmund's rival. That was more than my husband could tolerate. A vitriolic exchange of letters between the two men broke once and for all what had been a close six-year relationship.

"It took a lot longer than I had ever imagined" sighed Minna, with relief, "but at least Sigmund has finally come to his senses!"

I didn't share her sense of relief. On the contrary, what I found worrisome was a deeply depressed husband who was taking the separation extremely badly. For my part, I felt that Sigmund had been unfair to Jung. Moving forward from the position of son—dependent on Sigmund—was imperative for him. The time had come, I understood, for Jung to stand on his own two feet and found a new theory.

Their common interests had been few. In fact, I always wondered how those two could have gone on working together for such a long time. Jung's penchant for occultism was serious, his commitment, total. No one, not even Sigmund, could make him abandon it. His wife, Emma—a lovely and intelligent woman—wrote a letter to Sigmund that angered my husband greatly. Did Sigmund own the psychoanalytical field all by himself? she asked. Why couldn't Jung go about his own research without infuriating Sigmund? Did Sigmund have to be the only one, always? All these points made sense to me.

Meanwhile Ferenczi, who for quite some time had patiently been working on regaining his position, took instant advantage of the rupture to insinuate himself back into Sigmund's grace. Of Sigmund's close entourage, I have to say,he was always most pleasant to me, the only one with whom I had real conversations, all of which I enjoyed. But his servility to and perpetual adoration of Sigmund became unbearable to me. And despite his valiant efforts, Ferenczi never replaced Jung in Sigmund's heart. Something was broken in Sigmund, and he would never put his trust in another man. I often wondered how it had been possible for Sigmund not to have seen the writing on the wall. His infatuation must have bordered on love. Could this be the reason that from then on Sigmund welcomed only women—worshiping ones—around him? In any case, only those who did not question his theories or concepts became part of his court.

After Ferenczi, in 1912, a new Sigmund-worshiper appeared. Pretty, young looking, with an unusual charm and strength at the same time, and a sensual mouth, Lou Andreas Salomé made her way to Bergstrasse. Having attended the Weimar Congress—where she and Sigmund had met—she had arrived in Vienna to study with him. It was obvious that Sigmund was totally under her spell, as were our children, including Anna. Although outwardly friendly—mostly in an attempt to impress Sigmund—Minna, however, kept her distance.

"Did you see how she dresses?" she fumed. "How she combs her hair? And how she is working at seducing Sigi? Frankly, he behaves like a college boy in love!" Looking closely, I could see what attracted Sigmund and angered Minna. Lou was indeed utilizing every tool she had: beauty, elegance, wit, intelligence, and an original mind. Whenever I glimpsed them in some deep conversation, Sigmund's expression showed fascination. Though married, Lou was also known for her famous lovers, Nietzsche and Rilke among them. All of Lou's attributes, as well as her reputation, had triggered an unprecedented jealousy in Minna. As for me, I won't deny my own mounting feeling of concern.

Until now—not counting Sigmund's original passion for me—his deep emotional involvements had been with three male colleagues, Breuer, Fleiss, and Jung, all of which ended extremely badly. As for the women around Sigmund, they had either been seductive or interesting, never both.

What stung me most deeply was learning that Madame Salomé and I were exactly the same age. The luminosity of her beauty, her flowing hair, her large bright eyes, her sensual lips, made for a perfect image of both strength and femininity. When she appeared wearing her fur coat, she looked like a lioness. Her vivacious nature pointed up my lack of one—inevitably making me look old, colorless, and devoid of beauty. While I was put off by her and distrusted her, I could not bring myself to dislike her. In fact, according to Sigmund, Lou apparently spoke of me in the kindest terms.

"Pure maneuver!" declared Minna. "Don't be swayed by these flatteries. It's nothing but a ploy to deceive both you and Sigmund. Her manipulation is aimed at forging ahead while your guard is down. Wait and see, there is no way she'll let go of Sigmund. She needs to add another famous man to her hit list!"

Being aware of Sigmund's strict views on women's morality, his infatuation for Lou, given her dissolute past, surprised me no end. It brought to mind a heartfelt sermon Sigmund had given me while we were engaged, when a friend of mine, not wanting to wait for marriage, had begun to sleep with her future husband. "I forbid you from seeing her any-

more!" he commanded. With Lou, however, all his precon-
ceived notions and principles had vanished. He was mesmerized. She could do no wrong.

Even many years later, when Lou had become a psychoanalyst and published several theoretical articles, few understood why Sigmund—so quick to anger and vehement in
opposition to those who didn't agree with him—did nothing
to counter them. Anything Lou wrote, however strange, incomprehensible, and different from my husband's own theories, was accepted without criticism. How did this square
with his unbending attitude vis-à-vis his other diciples—Jung
first and foremost—who dared deviate from the master's
teachings?

"You don't seem to understand that the reason Sigi
never comments on her work is precisely because Lou is a
woman analyst—therefore no threat, no rival, really. For
him, Lou represents a woman in love with him—and he
with her. If I were his wife, I would not tolerate her presence
in my house," Minna advised.

Overreaction, I now know. I believe that a deep friendship is all it really ever was. A serious correspondence between them was followed by Sigmund inviting Lou to spend
some time in our house, on the pretense of bringing her
closer to Anna, not only as an analyst but because he knew
that Anna was as fond of her as he was. Sigmund always encouraged Anna to have female friends, to the detriment of
potential male ones. He was also banking on the fact that
Lou, not questioning Anna's attachment to her father, would
recommend that Anna continue to stay at home, to focus on
psychoanalysis.

In 1912, returning from her vacation with my family in Wandsbeck, a bubbly Sophie announced her engagement to Max Halberstadt, who was eleven years older than she. Sigmund and I were pleased with her choice. A photographer, he came from a good family and was himself a good and decent man. Our children had all been free to choose their spouses. Sophie and Max were married the same year and went to live in Hamburg. With sadness in our hearts, we let our pretty "Sunday child," as Sigmund had named her, leave the nest, sad because we would truly miss her, but happy that she had found a man she loved.

As you can see, here we are already in 1912, and I have not had much to relate about this time. So little happened to me then, whereas for Sigmund it proved to be a rich and important period. Whenever I compare Sigmund's full life to the mediocrity of mine, I become terribly depressed.

But I don't want to linger any longer over these depressing thoughts. I bid you good-bye, dear Mary, and thank you again for your generous gift.

Martha F.

12

Other memories came flooding back to me while I was writing that last letter—more intimate memories, the kind I have not talked about to anyone and could not confide to Mary despite the closeness we had reached in our relationship. During that same period, I remember dreaming many times about Sigmund's good-looking young protégé. I too appeared in those dreams—young and desirable—the two of us in erotic situations that made me wake up each time in a state of near orgasm. Needless to say, each time I was dumbfounded and horrified. Where on earth did such embarrassing scenes—even in my dreams—come from? And at my age! The mere fact of fantasizing such images shocked me. And it was all the more bizarre because my sexual life had been over for more than a decade!

I have no idea whether that young man was Jung or not. If I found Jung handsome at the time, I certainly never felt any physical attraction to him—at least, none I was aware of. It's probably his name that projected the image, *Jung,* "young man." My own lost youth. And I was living among young people involved in love matters. All this took place just when Mathilde had announced her engagement. I remember being sensitive to what I perceived emanating from her then. Her listless look, a certain indolence about her, made me recognize the tension that desire creates. Being around my daughter in love made me happy, then pained. My own love life—much too brief—seemed so distant.

Well-buried memories began surfacing, taking me back to the time of my engagement, when Sigmund was all passion—for my soul, for my body—a time when he could not contain himself from a constant urge to hug, touch, and kiss me. I recall finding all his manifestations of love a bit too much. They frightened me. No one, certainly no man, had ever approached me that way. In those days, no young lady, at least from a proper family, was instructed in matters of either courtship or love. I grew up in total ignorance, which probably explains why I didn't really suffer from our separation during the years of our engagement. Living in a cocoonlike environment between my mother and my sister gave me a strong sense of comfort. Each day was fueled by a new declaration of love from Sigmund, and his need to share whatever was going through his mind. What more did I need? Life seemed perfect. Once I was married, I knew, this comfort zone would vanish. Sharing everything, including Sigmund's bed, and living alone with him was in store for me. That was a bit daunting, giving rise to mixed feelings, I remember, a combination of curiosity on the one hand—for all the mystery attributed to the act of marriage—and on the other a gnawing anxiety. As for Sigmund, he deplored having to wait for what he promised would give me absolute happiness. I usually nodded, without a clue as to what his words meant.

I recall our first night together, which was both confusing and unpleasant. It was in Lübeck, where we had stopped on the first leg of our honeymoon. My husband, older than me by five years—already a doctor—would assuredly know how to initiate me into the secrets of love. The truth of the matter was, I now believe, Sigmund was probably as anxious as me, which didn't help matters. It all happened hurriedly, awkwardly. I watched my new husband as if possessed by some madness, convinced he was about to faint right next to me. Before I knew it, though, it was over. None of it presented much interest to me; in fact, I found it rather painful. Such was the fate of all wives, I told myself. In any case, pleasure or no pleasure, wasn't the point to please one's husband?

"Please forgive me, my darling wife, I wanted you so much! I have waited so long for this moment!" Sigmund showed definite remorse for having behaved "like a beast!"

Fine. I had now become a woman. Was this the whole mystery of love? All the celebrations in the name of love I had read about made me think that perhaps I had missed something. I appeared pleased, and Sigmund, unaware of my disappointment, was beaming, relaxed, happy. Anyway, given my absence of carnal knowledge, I could not have anticipated anything different.

As time went on, Sigmund became calmer and more tender. Once I began enjoying his reassuring caresses, all fear of pain vanished, and our nightly rituals started being pleasurable. I must say, satisfying Sigmund gave me an enormous feeling of success. Each night, from then on, Sigmund took possession of my body. It was as though he had to check on his new property. In any event, we grew closer every day. Despite the fact that our relative degree of pleasure varied, his access to what was most intimate in me had made my man an integral part of me. I finally understood that the way our love had evolved was what created the bond between a man and a woman. And that new form of love had nothing to do with whatever I thought of when the word *love* came to mind. Of course, knowing I was the object of his desire and satisfaction gave me a new sense of self-esteem. The consummate pleasure I knew I was giving Sigmund made me feel that that was what love was all about, and it was his.

Thinking back to our first lovemaking, I ask myself a question I had never articulated before. I had arrived at our wedding night ignorant, a virgin. But what about Sigmund? We never spoke about it. Had he known other women before me? Had he, like many young men, visited these special places where women initiate young men in need of experience? Come to think of it, I find it amazing that we never brought the subject up. Or was Sigmund simply as chaste as I? He was thirty, yes, but judging by his awkwardness at the time, the more I think of it, it is entirely possible that I was his first woman.

None of which explains how—given Sigmund's clear physical pleasure in lovemaking—literally from one day to the next, he was able suddenly to put a complete halt to our marital closeness once Anna was born. Didn't Sigmund miss all that? He was, after all, only forty at the time. A dozen years later, shaken by my erotic dreams, I woke up realizing the full extent of our abnormal situation. There I was, sleeping next to my husband night after night, with only a fraternal hug, a kiss on the cheek, a friendly hand touching my arm, to remind me we were married. Many a night I made a faint effort to snuggle—to no avail. Sigmund was, or pretended to be, asleep, and I would return somewhat humiliated to my erotic dreams.

Around 1905, when Sigmund's *Three Essays on the Theory of Sexuality* had come out, my mother came to visit.

"I see that your husband is still interested in those things. Hasn't he gotten over them, at his age?"

As I remained silent, I could feel my mother's worried look linger on me. This kind of remark, demonstrating how little impressed she was, fueled Mother in her later years, justifying her distance from her son-in-law. How could I explain to her that Sigmund had not only not gotten over "those things," but that "those things" had in fact become fundamental elements, absolute criteria—his dogma? Not addressing that issue, or not accepting it, meant not being able to study with Sigmund. It all belonged to his books. My own sexuality, Sigmund's, "ours" in fact, was no longer discussed.

Strange how, sitting at my table, with my puzzle laid out in front of me, I automatically pick up a piece at random and find it fits perfectly!

13

You ask me, dear Mary, to talk about Vienna in the years I mentioned in my earlier letters. Freud's name goes hand in hand with Vienna, I know. Strange as it may appear, however, we were not the kind of Viennese the term generally evokes. For that Vienna, I suggest you read Arthur Schnitzler's novels. He chronicles perfectly—and much more accurately than anything I could write—the glitter of Vienna, the lively Vienna. We were quiet bourgeoisie, living a life whose universe was limited to what went on in Berggasse. No fan of the theater or concerts halls even in his youth, my husband had never frequented dancing spots or other places where one was liable to meet *Susse Madel*. Actually, whenever I picture Sigmund on a dance floor, I burst out laughing. No, Sigmund's world was strictly confined to his mind. Period. I am convinced that he could have worked and made his major discoveries anywhere. For me, Vienna was what it had been for my mother. Like her, I never really took to the city, always put off by its frivolous aspects. With all these negative feelings, however, I did spend the better part of my life in Vienna. And yet I couldn't help feeling German. My obsession for German orderliness and seriousness is in direct opposition to the *Schlamperei*—happy-go-lucky attitude—of most Viennese.

Our household, plus Sigmund's work, occupied each of us so fully, many of the important events of the time—such as the Secession, the impact of artists like Klimt, Schiele, Kokoschka, the *Wiener Werkstatte*, and more—didn't really touch us. They seemed to pass us by. God! We were such narrow-minded classicists, when I think of it! All the effervescence of the art world around us at the time offended us in its modernity. Sigmund, if pressed, would have declared that all art had in fact stopped at the end of antiquity. We were also oblivious of all political life. I realize now that had we been more alert, we could have gleaned some important wisdom for our future. Yes, of course we heard about the various strikes taking place all over the city, and about an important one, scheduled for the first of May. But since none of that seemed to concern us directly, we tended to dismiss it. What was happening in the family struck me as far more important. I was deeply immersed in our big move from 8, Theresienstrasse to 19, Berggasse. At the time, it took my all—to the point of making me oblivious to the serious anti-Semitic protests that were taking place throughout the city.

I liked our first home in Vienna, an affordable apartment in a nice-looking modern building near the Ring—a prestigious address we would never have been able to afford if it had not suffered from its sinister history. Our building, named Sahnhaus, had been built on the ashes of the Ring Theater, which had been destroyed by a fire in 1881 that resulted in several deaths. Superstitious and afraid of the ghosts said to haunt the place, people were unwilling to move there. As a result, in the hope of luring people, rents were made ridiculously low. It was also perfect timing for us: I was pregnant with my fourth child, and we needed more space. Berggasse was not too far from the Ring, but the area was considerably less elegant than our former neighborhood. One end of our back street led onto the bridge to Leopold-stadt, the Rembrandtstrasse—where I had spent much of my youth. Also nearby was the Tandelmarket, a rather miserable flea market I did my best to avoid. Our end of the street was much more acceptable. Our move had the advantage of keeping us in the vicinity of the Freud family, which was im-portant, since we frequently traded visits. Still, I remember being disappointed the first time I saw the place, finding the new construction rather ordinary. What irked me especially was the butcher shop, which stood right next to our entrance. And to add insult to injury, the butcher's sign, which was cheek-by-jowl with my husband's, also bore the name Sig-mund! Unbelievable as it may be, the butcher and Sigmund shared the same first name! We had to grin and bear it. But as with everything in life, we finally got used to it. Just as well, because we went on living at that address for nearly forty-seven years.

The move was a clear improvement for us on two levels. The new place was larger, and the rent was cheaper. A year later, when a three-room apartment became available on a lower floor in the same building, Sigmund moved his office down, thereby freeing up more living space. In 1908, when an apartment of similar size to ours next door became avail-able, he moved back up onto our floor again. After much piercing of walls, Sigi's brand-new office space emerged, contiguous to us. From that moment on, our family life and his professional life became one.

To move back in time for a moment: in 1889 an earth-shattering event occurred that startled and upset everyone, including the Freud family. Archduke Rudolf and his mistress Maria Vestera committed suicide, followed two years later by the murder of Sissi, the emperor's wife. These tragic events forced us to pay attention to the world outside. Personally, I was saddened for the emperor, to whom I had a childlike devotion. Subsequent events proved even more upsetting, though we were unable to measure their consequences at the time. When Karl Lueger, a notorious anti-Semitic Pan-German, was elected mayor in 1895, we for the first time became alarmed. His party, the Social Christian Party, was a sugarcoated offshoot of another, earlier antiliberal, anti-Semitic party, United Christians. For "Christian," read "Non-Jew." Anti-Jewish slogans became the norm for Lueger, aided and abetted by a colleague named Schonerer. While posing as a moderate, Lueger touted "Christianity"—and religion in general—promoting bourgeois values. His constituents ate it up. By slow degrees he rid himself of his more violently outspoken comrades and, aiming at gaining as many adherents as possible, emphasized his "Christian" role. In other words, the wolf had clothed himself in the garb of a Good Samaritan. His own party appeared moderate and responsible. Even we bought it. How could we not? When he died, all Vienna paid him homage. It is true that he had done a great deal for the city, with efficient social-political measures such as buying back private gas and electrical industries and using the profits to improve all twenty of the Viennese districts. Under his mayoralty, trams had become electrified; hospitals were being built, as well as sanatoriums and municipal baths. During his mandate, he undertook another project that went straight to the Vienneses' hearts: the creation of a wonderful green belt encircling the city. While all this was changing Vienna for the better, an underground group was, however, secretly developing Lueger's original political credo, quietly waiting for the right moment to bring it out into the open.

During these troubled and changing times, we Freuds went on with our lives in a kind of nonreality, relegating outside events to a backdrop. Even rumors of war that percolated through the town somehow managed to pass us by. How could we have been that deaf and that blind? Were we so immersed in our own daily lives, we couldn't see beyond them? Whatever it was, the embarrassing fact remains that we never saw the war coming! The minutiae of our daily lives had blinded us completely: Sigmund and Jung's professional problems; Sigmund's ever-growing circle of adoring students; Sophie's wedding preparations—all seemed to be at the center of our preoccupations. I remember in detail the fabric of Sophie's wedding dress, and the endless hours it took for us to decide on our choice, the monogrammed sheets for her dowry, the menu for her wedding. The way we dressed in those days is also still vivid in my memory—rather like the fashion of my youth—with bustiers, waistlines accentuated by punishing corsets, wide hats with feathers or flowers. The basic difference was, our ankles were now showing, with shorter skirts! Gone were the multiple layers of petticoats. Also, our hairdos were no longer tight, pulled back in a chignon, but loosened, combed with artificial volume, giving us a softer look. Looking back, I'm ashamed to admit that these frivolities were then at the forefront of our minds.

Yet had we been just a trifle more vigilant, there were so

many ominous signs that would have worried us. In 1908, a revolution had occurred in Turkey. The fall of the Ottoman Empire offered Austria the possibility of annexing Bosnia-Herzegovina, and also allowed Bulgaria to declare its independence. All this was followed by a Balkan war, in 1912 and 1913, which dismantled European Turkey once and for all. A mercilessly deadly war, but that we learned only later. Serbian Slavs were beginning to stir. The papers were filled with news of all sorts of new alliances—hostile to us and Germany. Of course I never read the papers. If Sigmund did, he made no mention of it.

It's so odd. Apart from the deep hurt Jung had caused him, Sigmund's world for the most part remained peaceful. Psychoanalysis was penetrating many countries, new psychoanalytical societies were springing up as if overnight, and patients were coming in droves from around the world to see him. Having left his office downstairs, Sigmund was now receiving patients in his second-floor office, across from our apartment. As for me, I was basking in Sigmund's glory while pursuing my role as mother, as hostess to his mother and sisters on Sundays, directing and arranging everyone's vacation. Sigmund's daily walks were never interrupted, nor were his cigar-buying habits, his Saturday afternoon game of tarot cards with old friends. His Sunday morning ritual of bearing flowers to his mother went on as before, as did his Wednesday evening meetings at the Psychoanalytical Society. And then there were the biweekly sessions at the B'nai B'rith, the Jewish club to which he belonged. Our life seemed set, punctuated by its regular landmarks, dominated by Sigmund's total involvement in his writing, work, and ever-increasing correspondence.

* * *

In 1913 a slight change took place in the dynamics of our family—a change that would be the harbinger of something important to our future. Anna, almost eighteen, made a serious entrance on the scene. Her attachment to her father, unlike any he had ever experienced with the other girls, enveloped him and, indeed, filled him with joy. Very soon he became dependent on that new attachment. Both Mathilde and Sophie were married and out of the house by then. I noticed that whenever Anna left for vacation, Sigmund sank into a mild depression and complained that he was obliged to remain with only his "two old girls" for company. A joke of course, but I could nonetheless read between the lines.

It was obvious that Anna reciprocated Sigmund's feelings. As a young child, Anna had already captured her father's affection as none of the other children had. Her mischief, her frankness, often aggressive, always enchanted Sigmund. I still recall how hard Sigmund laughed one day when, after Mathilde had finished eating some apples two-year-old Anna wanted, the little girl ran to her father begging him to open Mathilde's belly to extract the apples for her. Growing up, Anna proved an excellent student. But that Anna was intellectually adept, that she wrote extensively—even poetry—were not the only elements that brought her close to Sigmund. Early on, Anna showed sincere interest, even passionate at times, in her father's work, and was forever asking all manner of questions about psychoanalysis. As time went on, she and her father would launch into lengthy discussions on the subject.

"Of course! The clever little thing! What better way to be appreciated by Sigi! She certainly has found the key to his heart!" Minna would grumble bitterly.

I refrained from reminding Minna that, not too far back, she too had used these tactics with her brother-in-law. Still, seeing how Anna, this young sprite of a girl, was invited to participate in all of Sigmund's activities did surprise me, to say the least. Sigi went so far as to having her accepted as auditor at the Wednesday meetings of the Psychoanalytical Society. But when Sigmund asked Anna to accompany him to America, it was greeted by a general outcry—the girl was only fourteen, for goodness sake! In retrospect, I can't understand how Sigmund could even have thought of it. But Anna did not have to wait long. As soon as she reached the age of seventeen, off she went traveling with her father. Whenever they were not together, a long, tender, and passionate correspondence sprang up between the two, Anna sharing her most intimate thoughts with her father. In a word, Anna had replaced Minna. Like a younger version of Minna, she had become a kind of colleague-cum-travel-companion to Sigmund. But this time, the bond of flesh and blood united them. Without anyone judging, of course: above all suspicion, Sigmund could lean on her with an affection he could never before have displayed with anyone else.

Despite all this open admiration and love from her father, I noted that Anna nonetheless seemed unhappy, slightly unbalanced emotionally. An extreme introvert, she opened up only in the presence of her father. Everything gravitated around Sigmund, who had become the absolute center of her life. Being who he was, Sigmund was fully aware of the situation, and should have seen to it that a necessary distance be made between them. All he really wished, he claimed, was for Anna to have a normal life as a woman, to get married like her sisters. His behavior, however, completely contradicted his declarations. How would this little girl ever find it in herself to leave the nest? Minna and I lamented to each other. But nothing I or Minna could say carried any weight with Anna. She had long ago stopped sharing her thoughts or feelings with any of us, having given her devotion to Sigmund and him alone.

In 1914, to illustrate how oblivious we were to what was happening in the outside world, we let Anna travel to England on July 18, shortly after the Sarajevo assassination of June 28! Again, I am still baffled that nothing outside our family seemed of any importance to us. We regarded any incident—no matter how serious—as just one more current event, no more significant than Sissi's assassination sixteen years earlier. Anna was supposed to spend several months with her uncles in Manchester and travel to the south of England with Loe Kann, Sigmund's ex-patient, whom she had befriended. Loe Kann was the first of Anna's women friends for whom she had developed a passion.

And then, to our shock and surprise, war was declared and all borders shut tight, leaving Anna in enemy territory. With the Austrian ambassador's help, she was able to travel through Gibraltar, Malta, and Genoa, and finally home to Vienna. Brave, even proud, Anna thrived, finding the adventure exhilarating and edifying. It is true that, unlike her older sisters, she had early on shown daredevil, tomboy qualities, much preferring to play games with Martin or swim and sail. As she became an adult, all lingering vestiges of coquetry vanished for good. It had become clear to us all that Anna was not seeking any life male companion. "Why should she look for a man? Doesn't she already have hers?" Minna proclaimed. Also, unlike most women at the time, and certainly unlike her sisters, Anna was intent on becoming a professional. In 1914, after enrolling in college and graduating with her teaching degree, she became a schoolteacher, to Sigmund's delight.

The assassination in Sarajevo affected me profoundly. One more member of the emperor's family brutally struck down—the heir to the throne, in fact. Still, I saw it as only one more episode in the tragic history of the royal family. Sigmund didn't seem to find it worrisome.

Sigmund's brother Alexander was the only one in our family who took Sarajevo very much to heart, predicting it would trigger dire consequences—which it did. But since we were all used to Alexander's rather pessimistic nature, none of us took his concerns too seriously. In our own blissful ignorance of international affairs, we had no clue that the murder of Ferdinand was the spark that would set off the war. In my innocence, how could I know that Serbian politics was endangering the Slavs' possessions in Austria-Hungary? Sure enough, the Austro-Hungarian Empire immediately gathered its might in a punitive offensive. Due to the alliances formed in previous years, a conflict that under normal circumstances might have remained at the local level set ablaze the entire continent. The emperor called for full mobilization, asking his people to rally to the defense of the fatherland and the monarchy. The response was swift and positive.

Everyone—including us—responded patriotically and emotionally to the declaration of war. I remember being surprised at our aggressive patriotism. As for Sigmund, he felt deeply for the first time what it meant to be Austrian. Interestingly, the fierce anti-Semitism expressed by every minority, the Serbs in particular, rebelling against the central government, made the Austrian and German anti-Semitism pale in comparison. The Russians—members of the enemy coalition—were the worst. As for France, that country remained an unknown entity for us. Like all Austrians, we obviously shared the wish that our country triumph over its adversaries. The only conflict, I recall, was in how difficult we found it to count England among our new adversaries. Sigmund had long considered England a role model, ranking at or near the top of his pyramid of nations. Furthermore, several members of our family already lived there.

Our sons left for the army, chins high. Martin, who had always looked up to those wearing the uniform, and to military life in general, was delighted to be drafted. He and his brother Ernst were immediately dispatched to the Galician front. Oliver was sent to various construction sites until he was finally enrolled as an officer in the army engineers. We were not unaware of the dangers they faced, but in some strange self-blindness—about which I ponder still today— neither Sigmund nor I was particularly worried about them. The joy and fervor with which the three of them left convinced us they had gone off on some exciting adventure. This feeling was corroborated each time they came home on leave, as none of them ever complained about a thing. What risk or danger could there be? It all seemed so positive. Ignorance has its virtues. And the war would be over soon, we kept telling ourselves. Fate dealt us a relatively good hand— nothing serious did happen to any of them, except for Martin. Being the most foolhardy of the three, in 1915 he was wounded and taken prisoner in Italy. After Ernst fell ill with pneumonia in 1916, the army sent him back from the front, and he finished the war in various hospitals and sanatoriums in the Tatras. Sophie's husband, Max, who was fighting in France, was also wounded and sent home. But all in all, the family was blessed with relatively few casualties. The war was being fought outside our borders, and our national propaganda made certain we saw little of the real picture. And so in the early months, the war unfolded with a false sense of distance for us. The Freuds quietly went on with their routine.

With some guilt, even shame, I must confess to having lived through the early months of that war with a kind of happiness. How can that be? I wonder today. Very selfishly, I welcomed the new circumstances that had brought me again close to my husband. A sense of new security enveloped me. Because trips were no longer possible, Sigmund was always home. Again, for the same reasons, visitors could no longer come and intrude on Sigmund's time. It reminded me of how, as a child, when traveling alone with my parents, I felt the full impact of our intimacy and security, seated together in the train compartment, protected from any intruder.

First months, then years went by while we pursued our daily routine, confident of an imminent victory. Sigmund's patients had become so scarce, he was able to devote more time to his writings, conferences, and correspondence. Everything else continued as before the war, including our summers outside Vienna. While Sigmund complained at not being able to travel—something he had loved and counted on before—for me it was pure bliss. Under the illusion of having won my husband back—all to myself—I was looking forward to continuing, once the war was over, a similar life, in which we lived close to one another, free of passion but wiser and happier. The solid stone walls of our Bavarian summer farmhouse kept us protected and uninformed. Nothing penetrated, making us impervious to what was going on outside those walls. Neither the mud of the trenches nor the stench of blood and death from a war that was decimating and sacrificing an entire generation seeped through to us. Nor did we have any inkling of what was to come in the not too distant future.

First, financial problems hit us. Our savings were melting like snow under the sun. The earnings from Sigmund's few Hungarian patients no longer sufficed. America had entered the war against us, and things quickly went from bad to worse. Food evaporated, coal supplies dwindled, and we suffered both hunger and cold—a situation that afflicted the entire country. In our naïveté, we reconciled ourselves to being hungry and cold as our way of participating in the war efforts. "Things will improve the minute war is won!" we told ourselves. Alexander-the-Pessimist, however, kept insisting that the Alliance would be defeated. Sigmund kept on with his research and work, but the shortage of tobacco upset him, along with an inflammation of his palate, which he neglected—the start of the illness that would ultimately kill him.

On November 21, 1916, our wonderful emperor Franz-Joseph died. It was a terrible blow to the whole nation, and a personal one for us. He had been a constantly reassuring father figure during all my years in Vienna. Franz-Joseph had overseen the destiny of our country for sixty-eight years. None of us had any idea that his death would in fact be the prelude to the Hapsburg Empire's dislocation—a determining factor that would plunge the country into chaos. We knew he had become weaker in recent years, but he had nonetheless always maintained order between the disparate members of his empire. When his nephew Charles I succeeded, the country felt the immense difference: compared to his uncle, he was clearly a lightweight.

Our horizon suddenly darkened. We had entered the last phase of the war. On May 17, Sigmund celebrated his sixty-first birthday, and despite my own anxiety, I made certain not to remind him of his superstition—sixty-one, he had declared, would be the age of his death! He did not mention it, and I was careful not to remind him.

That year was marked by a series of deaths. When Herman, Rosa's son, was killed at the front, it brought it all home. Only then did we fully measure the danger our own sons had been in all this time. The true horror of the war hit us for the first time.

The defeat had a devastating effect on all of us. I couldn't decide what exactly was at the base of our general depression. Our financial problems? The obvious humiliation of having lost? Something more profound? In any case, Sigmund became morose and somber, like someone who had lost all his points of reference, his landmarks.

Meanwhile, a great deal was going on in the world—and quite fast. The victors were parceling out the remains of the empire. One after the other, the countries that had been part of the monarchy seceded. New countries were born, leaving Austria small, without any of its previous resources, and dominated by an overly large capital. On November 10, 1918, Charles abdicated. The country became a republic, soon to be run, starting in 1920, by Social Democrats.

Known to history as the "Red Vienna," it would be constantly torn by conflicts up until the next war.

A shortage of everything plagued the country. Meat especially seemed to be what Sigmund missed most. Through the Red Cross, Sigmund's English relatives were able to complement our meager supplies by sending us precious packages—none, alas, really appeasing our hunger. With his emaciated face, his beard turned gray, a frail silhouette, Sigmund had suddenly turned the corner; for the first time, he looked old. The winter of 1918–19 was bitter cold and extremely harsh. The absence of coal for our furnace made it impossible for Sigmund to work at his desk. On the other hand, inflation was raging. Taking care of our own household and that of his mother and sisters had become increasingly problematic for Sigmund. The insurance policy Sigmund had taken out in my name—100,000 crowns—was barely enough for a taxi fare. As did most people, we found ourselves as poor as on the first day of our marriage.

Immigration was on a lot of our friends' minds. Jones suggested England; Sachs and Pfister, Switzerland; Ferenczi, Hungary—all of which Sigmund summarily rejected. Leaving his Vienna was simply impossible. Even twenty years later, as he gradually came to grips with the world, he had trouble deciding to leave his city. No one could figure what in the world had kept Sigmund there, since he had long ago openly declared that he had lost all respect for both Austria and Germany. As far as I was concerned, despite my attachment to this relatively recent country of mine, nothing could have made me stay in a place I knew to be unsafe for our family. But no one asked for my opinion on the matter.

Sigmund's principal, and urgent, focus was to find new

patients, preferably American and English, who could pay him in foreign currencies. Thanks to Jones, who as soon as the borders opened up again recommended a few British patients to Sigmund, we were once again able to make ends meet. And thanks to good word of mouth, Sigmund's patients started arriving in ever-growing numbers. Like so many, we had been lucky, having come out the other side alive! Had we not paid each in his own personal way our dues to fate? Wasn't it time for better days?

Better days seemed to have finally come our way. Our sons got settled back into their respective lives. All three married, and grandchildren soon followed. It looked as if we could now enjoy the bounties around us. Life with its infinite promises seemed at long last to be smiling on us. But I rejoiced too soon. After the dreadful toll of the war, a terrifying flu epidemic ravaged all of Europe. It hit us where it hurt most: our Sophie became one of its victims, dying the following January, on the twenty-fifth, to be exact, leaving us completely devastated. A few days before, a close friend of Sigmund's, Anton von Freud, had also died.

But death had just begun its relentless march. In 1920 Mitzi lost her husband. In 1922 Rosa's daughter Cecilie committed suicide at the age of twenty-three, the following year Mitzi's son Teddy drowned in Berlin, and at roughly the same time I also learned of the death of my brother Eli in America. The list of casualties went mercilessly on. Sophie's second son, Heinerle—raised by Mathilde after Sophie's untimely death—a child Sigmund adored, perished from a form of virulent tuberculosis. Sigmund and I were with him until the end. I will never forget the poor child's horrible agony. This last loss undid Sigmund completely.

Just a few weeks earlier, Sigmund's cancer had declared itself. The timing of it all destroyed us. For the next sixteen years, Sigmund's existence became a calvary.

I am so tired. And sick unto death. Once again I have digressed, not addressing your question, and instead let myself be tempted into the past. If it led me back to that terrible World War I, you must understand that it was for us, like so many others, a rupture, a turning point. Nothing was ever the same after that war.

Tonight I no longer have the strength to go on. The New Year is approaching, and according to convention, may I offer you my warmest and best wishes? I must confess, the end-of-year celebrations don't have the same appeal they once had. No doubt my ripe old age has something to do with my apathy.

I send kisses,

Martha F.

14

I am not sure whether or not it is the New Year, with its perennial and absurd list of good intentions, but today I set about assiduously rearranging my drawers and closets. Anyway, it has been far too cold to go out.

In the course of going through my papers, I came upon the pack of letters Sigi had sent me during our engagement, and felt compelled to reread them. All the more incomprehensible that to date I had scrupulously avoided delving back into these bygone times. True, early on, when I began feeling abandoned by Sigmund, rereading those passionate letters had a way of refueling me. I needed to grab onto any confirmation I could that he loved me. These letters were my source of renewed adrenaline. As the years went by, however, their content seemed so far removed from the reality of my life that I stopped opening them. It was as if that onetime treasure had lost its value.

Reading that correspondence today confirmed to me once again that they had indeed been thought through, and were written with me in mind. Now, however, they failed to have their desired effect. The very lines that had once ignited my passion read like those of a novel. What in the world was I doing? The Martha these letters had been addressed to was no longer the same woman. The man who had signed them seemed distant, a stranger. Tying the knot on the pack of letters, I put them away. What was the point? Did I need to remind myself I had once been the object of Sigmund's love, all those many years ago? I had never forgotten that. Can an entire life be built on just a few years of love? Anyway, I'm not even sure why I kept them. In fact, I must think about destroying them. Were they to fall into a stranger's hands, I would be completely mortified.

Anxious for more about my past, I pulled out some photo albums and started looking through them, focusing on my youth, lingering over pictures of my mother, Minna, and me, without any sentimentality, only curiosity. All that seems so far away now. The one photograph that did capture my attention was of me standing next to Sigi, at the time of our engagement. Sigmund is seated, the upper button of his coat stitched together, his right sleeve forming pleats at his shoulder. His coat, buttoned high, hides his tie, as was the fashion of the time. I am standing to Sigmund's left, my right hand resting on his shoulder, my fingers clenched; rather stiff, my hair pulled back into a chignon. My expression is calm, without a trace of a smile. The light-colored dress I am wearing is ugly, complicated with its pleats and draping. Not particularly flattering, but probably the best I had in those days. In any case, we are both staring at some identical point, both looking serious, with proper composure. Nothing in the picture reveals, even hints at, the passion contained in our letters. Seeing again the handsome young man with his deep look, the trusting fiancée I then was, with this air of happiness for the future in her eyes, touched me immensely.

Destiny. In my letters evoking the past years, I often asked myself why on earth our life had turned so irreversibly dark. Would the void carved by the war always remain huge, with death tolling ad infinitum? It all seemed incomprehensible. I sometimes asked myself, What had we done to incite God's wrath? On the brink of slipping into a world of superstition, I felt ready to follow any astrologist at the drop of a hat. That endless ordeal struck me as both incomprehensible and absurd. I was ready to accept virtually any explanation, however dubious. At least it would have soothed my troubled mind. No point in sharing these thoughts with Sigmund. All this is without rhyme or reason. I knew what he would have said: There is no god to blame! The sky was forever empty. I was left more desperate than ever, more alone.

I noted that our trials and tribulations seemed merely to add fuel to Sigmund's atheism. On the one hand, there I was, unable to share my sadness; on the other, Sigmund, weathering it all with exemplary dignity and courage. Where did he find his strength? In the state of mind I was in, I sometimes said to myself that the only explanation was his outsized sense of pride. In a way, I would have welcomed his being less strong, closer to me, in these cruel moments.

When we emerged from the war, Sigmund admitted to having been horribly wrong about everything: Austria, Germany, the meaning and outcome of the conflict—but mostly about mankind. He was stricken by this self-revelation. The future looked irrevocably bleak for him. Death had become his constant preoccupation. Again, in my infinite and incurable naïveté, I had believed that all the sad things we had lived through would bring us closer together. How wrong I was! Sigmund's intensified work became his sole refuge. And when his old students reappeared, he spent most of his time preoccupied by psychoanalysis and its growing importance worldwide.

In March 1919 I was felled by a terrible pneumonia, which left me incapacitated for several months. In July, while I was still recovering, Sigmund and Minna left together for Bad Gastein, a thermal spa town, a yearly habit that went on for the next four years. Probably because of my weakened health, I felt completely abandoned after they left. By the time they returned, however, feeling somewhat recovered, we all left to visit Sophie in Hamburg, the last time we would see her.

The following year I accompanied Mathilde, who was ill, to Ischl, while Sigmund and Minna returned to their thermal baths. Later on that summer, Sigmund took Anna with him for a visit to our son-in-law—now a widower—and his children. The fact that Sigmund had not spent a single day with me that summer didn't affect me in the least. We were all shattered by Sophie's loss. Nothing had any importance or meaning for me. Everything had changed forever. Our beloved daughter was no more. Ernst and Oliver had moved to Berlin, and while Mathilde and Martin still lived in Vienna, they were both married, and we saw relatively little of them. The big Berggasse apartment was now left with only four residents, Sigmund and three women: Minna, Anna, and me. By now our respective roles had changed. Anna had become the perfect colleague for Sigmund, and with her he shared his professional thoughts and ideas. It was with her, too, that he relaxed. Their complicity, their mutual love, were there for all to see, including me of course, who was understandably jealous. Realizing this, I was forced to question my reaction. How could a mother harbor feelings of jealousy toward her daughter? Shouldn't this ideal display of filial devotion and affection rather elicit my admiration?

What was my problem? There was something wrong with the picture. But after all my self-questioning, the fact remained: Yes, indeed, I was jealous! I had good reason for it, as the future would prove.

As for Minna, she had not yet been completely dethroned and still enjoyed a fair amount of Sigmund's company. Less sprightly than before, she often needed to absent herself from the house to take various cures. As for me, I was left with virtually nothing for Sigmund to share. Or at least, nothing of any importance. Relegated firmly to the role of attendant or maid, I still looked after Sigmund's clothes and prepared his morning bath, positioning his toothpaste tube to make it easy for him to press. (How embarrassing!) I helped him get dressed each morning, and all in all played the role of an old relation taken in by charity—a relation Sigmund felt responsible for, one he surely wouldn't abandon. What remained of our relationship was a mere echo of distant affection. The only one capable of igniting pleasure in Sigmund was Anna. Very simply, she had become indispensable.

In September 1920, Sigmund asked Anna to accompany him to a psychoanalytical congress in the Hague, the first after the war. This trip represented Anna's official entry into the world of psychoanalysis. The mere fact of her being with and next to Sigmund, in the presence of his students, had anointed her his official heir. At the closing banquet of the conference, Anna apparently delivered a brilliant speech in English, which was received with a standing ovation.

"How do you imagine people, in that context, not applauding the master's daughter?" remarked Minna with her usual bitterness. From that moment on, Minna kept an eagle eye on Anna's every move, sparing no comment or criticism, always discreetly, for us two alone.

And so father and daughter carried on their increasingly close relationship, discussing professional matters, traveling together. Sigmund had merely changed partners—this time letting Minna drop and promoting Anna. After their trip to Holland, Anna went on to Hamburg to take care of her orphaned nephews. All Minna had enjoyed with Sigmund until then was a thing of the past. Reluctantly, she resigned herself to passing the mantle on to her younger, more professionally able successor.

I believe I was more jealous of Anna than I had been of Minna. And I was certainly far more hurt by the complicity that united Anna and her father. With Minna, it had been different. She was my sister, a woman of my generation, with whom I shared a lifelong bond despite the ongoing rivalry. As for Anna, we lived in two separate worlds. I was also aware that there was no way I could match her psychoanalytical expertise, which daily brought her closer to Sigmund. Although superficially she showed respect for me, the absence of any tenderness, her lack of intimacy, was blatant. Nothing compensated the resentment she inspired in me. I can't help but think I was being repaid in kind for having neglected—perhaps even rejected, in her early years—that child I never wanted.

I didn't embrace the many women colleagues gravitating around Sigmund, with the exception of Helene Deutch, who made a big impression on me. Of Polish origin, she was a brilliant woman doctor who, after undergoing analysis with Sigmund, went on to make a major impact within the psychoanalytical community. Her husband, Felix, became Sigmund's physician, and I thus got to see her quite often. Endowed with great intelligence and energy, she was also an extremely elegant woman. After being invited by Sigmund to become a member of the Wednesday Psychoanalytical Society and pursuing her own analysis in Berlin with Karl Abraham—who, it is said, fell madly in love with her—she returned to Vienna to practice.

Having this type of very accomplished woman in his entourage was a new phenomenon for Sigmund. While Helene impressed him, his attachment to her did not remotely resemble his earlier closeness to Lou. Lou represented the opposite of Helene—an idealist bohemian, poetic, always broke—all of which elicited Sigmund's protective instincts. Helene was solid, her feet firmly on the ground at all times. She never wavered from her goal, which was to succeed in everything she did or planned to do. Something else set her apart from all his other women students: her attitude was that of an independent, strong colleague rather than an adoring and cowed student. I even wondered at times whether she wasn't around Sigmund merely to further her own career. Wasn't belonging to the inner circle a sure recipe for success? In any case, Helene wasted no time fawning or displaying worship, as had her predecessors.

Be that as it may, aware of who she was, although our lives had surely little or nothing in common, starting with our respective husbands (hers was adoringly at her feet), I couldn't help being awed by that woman. It was clear that in that couple she ran the show. I think that in my heart of hearts I envied her. She represented everything I would have liked to have been: beautiful, strong, independent, educated, creative . . . and free! None of these thoughts had of course been as clearly formulated within me at the time as they are today, but they undoubtedly explain my attraction to this paragon of success. She was such a contrast to my simple, unambitious self.

In 1935, alarmed by the growing Nazi threat—and ignoring Sigmund's accusation that she was deserting him— Helene immigrated to America. I'm happy to know that Mary underwent analysis with her. I'm sure she was the best analyst available.

Helene's psychoanalytical focus was women, a specialty not yet popular in the 1920s, and one of little interest to Sigmund. He prided himself on applying his theories fairly to both sexes. I remember wondering whether the Oedipus complex—of which Sigmund was a prime example—could be something I unconsciously suffered from as well. So many unanswered questions. Had Sigmund asked me go undergo analysis, I know I would have jumped at the opportunity. But that was out of the question. It was far easier for him to classify me as "normal"; no psychoanalysis was imaginable for me in either his or my eyes. This said, much later I recognized clear echoes of what concerned me in his work.

"Your puzzle isn't making much progress, madam!" exclaimed Paula as she brought my herbal tea. It is true that since starting this correspondence and my journal, there simply has been little or no time for my puzzle these days. Instead of assembling the missing puzzle pieces, however, am I not doing virtually the same thing, filling in pieces of memory, hoping it will all fit in the end?

Darkness has descended. A perfect silence covers the

obscurity. What am I going to do? It's much too early for my bedtime. Yet how cozy my bed would be, with its folded-over sheet and warm down comforter. But the prospect of lying awake for hours with my eyes open is unbearable. Images of the long evenings reading in bed, all these many years ago, waiting in vain for Sigi to come up and inevitably falling asleep on my book with the light still on, flash back to me. Better if I go to read in the easy chair. No point in waiting up for someone to join me—that is a thing of the past. Lying in my bed now would make the silence all the thicker, more ominous, whereas sitting in an easy chair gives me the illusion that I can get up anytime, even flee if I feel like it. Flee from what, exactly? Not the bombings, surely. It was something else. Was it fleeing from my dreams, my threatening dreams? Perhaps the void, the huge void that awaits me.

Lately, I often dream that I am back in Wandbeck. It's wintertime, white and cold, and I glide, light and graceful, across our frozen pond. My muscles are in perfect harmony. I am perfectly happy until I catch my mother's reproachful stare at the edge of the pond. Startled, suddenly aware of having done something wrong, I wake up, my heart pounding.

My mother never disapproved of our ice skating. On the contrary, that healthful activity was encouraged in our family. Minna usually accompanied me, along with several friends and cousins, to enjoy these innocent, fun-filled pleasures. Later on, our children kept up the tradition, especially Mathilde, who loved skating in the rink at the Augarten. How I wish I could have joined my children! No, it was not my mother but Sigmund who had forbidden me to skate when we first met, I remember. The notion that I could be touching a young male ice skater while skimming around the rink, or—even worse—that he could be holding me by the waist, was more than he could bear! Finished were my days of waltzing on ice. Why on earth did I let myself be deprived of something that brought me so much pleasure? What indeed had been the matter with me?

15

Maresfield Gardens
January 15, 1947

My dear Mary,

Many thanks for your package, which arrived today, and everything it contained, which the entire household is enjoying. Please forgive me for sharing the sweets with the young English ladies working for us. They are far more deprived than we, and never complain. I never cease admiring the English for their extraordinary dignity in the face of suffering and deprivation. I thank you on their behalf. As for Paula, nothing could have pleased her more than your cans of corned beef. And real eggs! — she could no longer bear the taste of powdered eggs. I must scold you, however, for the extravagant shawl of soft blue-gray wool that you sent. It hasn't left my shoulders since I opened your package. I love it. Everyone is overwhelmed by it. Anna insisted on finding who had sent me this royal gift. I replied with a white lie, telling her it came from my sister-in-law, whose name is also Anna. Pitiful lie! That Anna would never have given me such a gift, any more than my daughter would. Anyway, Anna frowned and bought my lie, or pretended to.

I must ask you to stop sending me these wonderful packages, simply because I'm afraid I won't be able to hide the identity of the sender much longer. And as you know, keeping our epistolary relationship secret is important, nay, essential. Saying which, I thank you from the bottom of my heart for treating me in such a lavish way. How can I possibly reciprocate? Here, nothing belongs to me anymore. I am not permitted to touch any object in this house, particularly those belonging to the Freud Museum. While my husband left me the use of everything, I can't dispose of anything without consulting. Ever since Sigmund's death, I have been living under my children's jurisdiction. My hands, I'm sorry to say, shake these days. Otherwise I would embroider you a tablecloth, as I used to. Alas, that activity belongs to a distant past. Still, without promising any results, I shall try to knit you something.

In your last letter—as you have these past months—you asked me to answer some specific questions. Your curiosity regarding me is always so warm and genuine—as it has been since the outset of our letter writing—that responding to you and answering your questions have been a daily source of pleasure for me. Putting pen to paper for you was a new adventure, and something I always looked forward to. Oddly, though, something I was not prepared for struck me as I started writing you this time: in front of the blank white sheet of paper, I felt—the word is not too strong—nauseous. Utter disgust took over my whole being. Unable to write a single word, I got up from my chair as if I were being pursued by someone. The next few days I felt weak, overcome by an immense fatigue. Getting out of bed became almost impossible, to the point where Paula, alarmed, called Mathilde, who suggested calling the doctor. "Nonsense!" was my reaction. I wasn't sick, at least not physically. Was digging through my memories the source of my malaise? Or was my body simply reacting to one of the most painful moments of my life? I am referring to the time when I realized there was no turning back from the slow degradation leading to the final destination—death. Don't take me wrong. Old age, or even death, doesn't frighten me. I do shiver, however, at the notion of leaving a big void behind, a name without the slightest echo. I am not referring to the name "Freud"— which has now become immortal, and belongs to my husband. I am referring to me—Martha—whose existence amounts to absolutely nothing. The worst thing is being painfully aware that the "nothing" I accuse myself of representing is my own doing. A rather long tirade, I am afraid, merely to explain why I didn't properly reply to your last letter.

All this brought to mind an incident that occurred in 1923, when I first became aware that I didn't matter much to anyone in my family. The New Year was approaching, and bringing everyone together seemed the right thing to look forward to. Our financial situation had improved; the whole country was getting back on its feet, with even some signs of prosperity. Lucy had just given birth, and Ernst and Lucy had been unable to join us—traveling with a three-week-old baby was out of the question for them. With my inevitable mother-in-law, my widowed sisters-in-law, Alexander, his wife, and their three children, we were eighteen. The sight of his grandchildren had always pleased—indeed overjoyed— Sigmund. He had a special passion for little Heinerle, Sophie's second son, who I must admit was an adorable little fellow. His older brother Ernst—less charming—had no doubt been more affected by the loss of his mother. Anna, taking matters into her own hands, was practicing some of her psychology on her nephew. She had left her teaching career and was now fully involved in a pedagogy inspired by psycho-analysis, principally aimed at emotionally disturbed children. Most of her little patients were children of psychoanalysts.

Everyone made a point of being merry that day, trying valiantly to ignore Sigmund's dark mood and Max's depression. Neither had recovered from Sophie's death. Mathilde had arrived a few days before, somewhat depressed. She shared her worry that her husband, Robert, was getting frustrated with her inability to have children. "How would you feel," she asked, "if I were to adopt Heinerle?" I personally thought it was a fine idea, for several reasons. First, Mathilde really wanted to become a mother, and this seemed a perfect opportunity. Second, Heinerle needed the love of a mother. Third, if Heinerle lived with Mathilde—whose apartment was close to us—Sigmund would be rewarded with frequent visits from one of his favorite grandchildren. I doubted that Max, who was overwhelmed by his loss and seemed to have lost all taste for life, would object.

Contemplating the assembled group, and my daughters-in-law in particular, I marveled at how different their lives were, compared to mine at their age. As they moved about the room, it was clear they were experiencing a new freedom. Even the way they dressed underscored the independence they were all enjoying. Gone were the constricting corsets of yesteryear, giving way to flowing dresses, shorter skirts revealing ankles, cropped hair, falling below the ears. Chignons under big hats were gone. Wearing their cute little felt cloches as hats, they moved about with a pixielike air. As for the men, each had shaved his mustache and looked far more comfortable in his suit. What also struck me was the change in the relationship between couples. And, of course, in none of these young women did I detect the unconditional depend-ence that had dominated my own life.

The new playing field, however, was not quite level with the old, I reminded myself. Take Lucy, for example: un-like me, she possessed a personal fortune, which would have enabled her to leave Ernst any time she pleased. What was more, I had no profession, while each of these attractive young ladies that day in my living room did, and could at any time—without people frowning—decide to go out and earn her own living. Musing about our differences, I was being rather conveniently shortsighted. Hadn't plenty of women in my day become emancipated, broken tradition, and become professionals? If I had left my mother's tight hold to fall di-rectly into my husband's, I had no one to blame but myself. Why didn't I free myself? Rebel? Was it weakness? A submis-sive personality? In any case, none of it seemed to give me a good enough reason to voice my discontent. My life had al-ways been decided by others, and that was that.

As usual, there was my mother-in-law, sitting up straight and proud in the middle of our living room with a self-congratulatory smile on her face, looking around at her brood as if it was all thanks to *her* good work—or, more prop-erly, that of Sigmund and her. In a flash, I caught the tableau in front of me. Sigmund was at the center, seated between his mother and Anna, holding Heinerle on his lap, the son of his lost daughter. Mathilde, close by, was eying the group with affection and a little envy, knowing that within days this little angel would be hers. Then my eyes fell on Minna, whose role, as we know, had been usurped by Anna, sitting without saying much, tight-lipped. Something else caught my eye. It was Ernst. Slightly hidden by his father, he was staring, sending daggers at his brother. Family! Family life with all its complexities and horror. I wasn't part of the tableau. An incredible sense of liberation took possession of me. This was the first time I felt relieved not to be part of it. In fact, I would never again want to be part of the tableau.

Letting my eye wander, I saw sons and sons-in-law chatting with Alexander. Farther on, there were hushed whispers among the daughters-in-law. Then there was the corner, with Sigmund's sisters Mitzi, Pauli, and Rosa—all three widows— huddled together around the fourth sister, Dolfi, and their mother, Amalia, looking a bit down and miserable. All four reduced to living off Sigmund. A ray of rage burned within me. Why did these Freud women not seek an education? How had they let their mother sacrifice them to allow their brother to pursue an education? And what about Sigmund? Didn't these old ladies, now dependent on his charity, make him feel tremendously guilty? How could it be that, despite his declarations of brotherly affection, he felt no contempt for them? Many years later, Sigmund—selfish man—thought little of leaving behind this sweet pack of sheep, so kind and admiring, abandoning them, leaving them defenseless, prey to Hitler. Harking back to that time, I can't help but be overcome with anguish and distress. But I prefer not to dwell on it. Not now.

Going through some photo albums recently, I came upon one picture in particular—I'd like to show it to you—taken the day of our twenty-fifth anniversary: September 14, 1911. I found it so terribly sad. Strange, how different an image can seem, depending on when one views it. In any event, I remember that day well. We had reserved a large reception room in Klobenstein for our celebratory dinner. Robert, Mathilde's husband, who is missing, must have been the one taking the picture. Only three sides of the table are occupied: Oliver, Ernst, Anna, and Sigmund are seated on the left, while on the smaller side, Mathilde and I are seated side by side. On the right side, I see Minna, Martin, and Sophie. A white tablecloth, flowers, napkins artfully folded, adorn the rectangular table. I find the composition of the picture interesting. Robert framed the picture, I am certain, with the idea of focusing on my husband, although Sigmund was not really seated in the middle. From that angle, Sophie was hiding Minna and Mathilde, making them nearly invisible. Martin is obviously stretching his neck to appear in the picture. As for me, I can barely spot myself at the darker end. As I see it, Anna, seated to Sigmund's right, makes it look as though the two of them are the couple being celebrated that evening. A sinister picture. Everyone looks made of stone. Not a smile in sight. Looking at that picture on the mantelpiece of my bedroom reminds me not to shed too many tears of regret for my life.

Coming back to that New Year's Day family reunion, I remember experiencing a kind of epiphany as I looked at Minna, my sisters-in-law, and myself. None of us had lived a meaningful life. All of us women of that generation had been systematically trained into being useless, prevented from realizing our potential selves. For so many years, I had pretended that everything was fine. Suddenly the charade of having been "an excellent housewife who had diligently overseen Sigmund's happiness" — as he had clearly stipulated before our marriage — choked me. Wasn't what everyone had termed "happiness" a euphemism for Sigmund's daily comfort? But as the provider of his happiness was concerned, I had been supplanted by others. I also recall, as I registered what I was seeing for the first time, feeling a migraine coming on and fighting it as best I could. Old acquaintances of mine, these bouts of migraines had started when I was a young girl, and returned in a serious way after Anna's birth, attacking me whenever I was faced with unpleasant thoughts or difficult situations. Sigmund had been unable to help, alas, except for advising me to drink linden tea. "Women are often prone to migraines!" was all my eminent doctor-husband had to offer. He was far more solicitous with his female patients suffering from bouts of hysteria. Sigmund assumed that all was well for me in that respect: either I was devoid of a subconscious, or it was not worth his time. When in 1900 aspirin came onto the market, Sigmund often prescribed it to me, and things improved. Subconscious or no subconscious, whatever that may mean, my migraines disappeared for good after Sigmund's death!

That New Year's Day, 1923, life had returned to the house. The sound of many voices once again echoed in our living room over the holiday, which pleased me greatly. Since five of our children had flown the coop, our house had fallen almost silent and lost much of its former effervescence. The only sound interrupting the silence had been the doorbell ringing each time one of Sigmund's patients arrived. It was always the same ritual: first, the patient was ushered into

Sigmund's office drawing room; then he or she entered his office, and I could hear the door close behind them. Three rooms now constituted Sigmund's office: his drawing room, his medical office, and his own working office with its big desk. I rarely penetrated that sanctuary except to verify it had been properly cleaned. Minna had taken over one of the children's rooms and turned it into her boudoir, now filled with embroidered cushions, lace doilies, and filigreed objects. One would have thought that in light of all the new space in the house, she would have moved altogether into more comfortable quarters. But no. The small space contiguous to ours where she had slept since the day she had moved in remained her bedroom of choice.

As for Anna, she now occupied an office next to that of her father, plainly furnished except for a portrait of Sigmund. Taking her new role of psychoanalyst very seriously, she, like Sigmund, had taken to remaining for hours behind closed doors, working.

Minna no longer lingered over manual work with me, preferring to repair to her quarters. Our meals were spent with little conversation to distract Sigmund from his preoccupations. Lately he had become somber, preoccupied, lost in his thoughts. And anyway, the exciting part of his life was taking place outside.

The assembled family exchanged good-byes, wishing everyone the best for the new year. None of us anticipated what was to come: the worst year ever.

I shall never forget that morning in April 1923. Each of us was busy—Anna in her office; Minna in the living room; and

I down in the kitchen, planning the week's menu. The phone rang, and Anna answered. Someone in Dr. Hajek's clinic, where Sigmund—unbeknownst to us—had apparently gone that morning, asked that we bring Sigmund's clothes for the night. For the night? Yes, they were keeping him overnight! Completely in the dark as to why, the three of us—Minna, Anna, and I—jumped into a taxi. Sigmund, it turned out, had been found to have a tumor in his palate, which they had told him was benign. It was a "minor intervention," and Sigmund didn't want to worry us. In any case, he had agreed to have it removed and was told he could return home the same day.

I shall never forget our following the nurse down the corridors, entering his room, and seeing Sigmund sitting in a chair, his face covered with blood. He was in horrible pain, unable to open his mouth. We were all in shock. What had happened? The "minor intervention" had turned out badly, and Sigmund had started to hemorrhage. Sigmund would have to remain in the clinic overnight for observation, the matron in the white frock told us. The problem was, there was no room available; all that was available was a chair. Sigmund had to remain seated in the chair throughout the night. Anna exploded in a rage; raising her voice, she told everyone in the clinic that this was "completely unacceptable," until finally a bed was improvised in a room already occupied by a dwarf, a retarded person who was there for God knows what. I don't know why, but the presence of this poor soul upset me more than anything. The nurse assured us that everything was under control and urged us to return home. Two hours later, we were back in the clinic. We learned Sigmund had had a second hemorrhage and had tried to ring for help, but the bell didn't function. His room-mate, the dwarf, had run outside to fetch a nurse. This time, Anna once again took charge and insisted on remaining in the room next to her father. I was sent home. There was no room for both of us.

Sigmund was sent home late the next morning. Anna was still beside herself. During the night Sigmund complained that he was in great pain, but when Anna asked the night doctor to help, he refused. As Sigmund was about to go home the next morning, Dr. Hajek insisted on bringing him to his students as a case study. Radiation was prescribed, along with radium medication—all of which was very painful. Bravely, despite his pain, Sigmund had not once complained.

I, however, was far less courageous. With no clue as to the nature of his illness, I was under the impression that we had not been told the entire truth. I was also mystified by the way the incident had unfolded—much too strangely, too incomprehensibly. Even today, as I relive the incident, the same bewilderment, the same disgust, takes hold of me. How could someone like Dr. Hajek—who, while not a close friend of Sigmund's, was nonetheless a distinguished colleague of his—have handled this operation so high-handedly? I find it also unbelievable that Sigmund would have submitted himself to such inhuman treatment. Why had he, the ultra-meticulous doctor, been so docile a patient, he who never let anyone decide for him? What power did Dr. Hajek hold over Sigmund?

Another odd, unexplained element about this whole affair remained murky for me. During all this time—and well after—the nature of Sigmund's illness was never clearly articulated. Only the term *benign tumor* was bandied about. It took months for the word *cancer* to finally be uttered. Sigmund, and others most likely, had had knowledge of his cancer. Early on, when Sigmund asked Felix Deutch, almost in passing, to "take a look at this unpleasant something inside my mouth that's been bothering me the past two months," Dr. Deutch sent him to a dermatologist, who upon seeing this hard, white spot, had diagnosed it as a "leukoplakia" and out of precaution urged surgery. Deutch immediately knew that it was cancer, and was devastated to learn it.

Sigmund, always wanting to spare his mother from suffering his death, had earlier come to an agreement with Deutch that, when the time came, Deutch would facilitate his exit from this world. Knowing this, Deutch was fearful that if my husband learned the true nature of his illness, he might commit suicide, and so he withheld the truth from him. After lamely turning Sigmund over to the dermatologist for the "minor intervention," he looked the other way. He was subsequently reproached for his medical laissez-faire. Had Deutch addressed the issue more professionally from the start, Sigmund would have been appropriately operated on by a serious oncologist. In the meantime, the secret was kept for several months. When Deutch brought the case to committee, they advised—God knows why—to maintain the silence. It was only after Sigmund's second operation, in October of that year, that his malady got its proper name.

Upon learning what he really had, Sigmund flew into a rage, asking, "What right did they have to hide the truth from me?" Who can I blame? Who was to take full responsibility for this catastrophic treatment? Dr. Hajek? Felix Deutch? Sigmund himself? Hadn't he, from the start, regarded his tumor with utter and incomprehensible lightness of heart, deferring all medical knowledge? Having noticed something unusual in his mouth as far back as 1917, why had he waited so long to see his doctor? That Sigmund assuaged his fears by going along with a dermatologist continues to mystify me. He later told me that he had been afraid another doctor would have forbidden him to smoke. I suppose his smoking was Sigmund's way of defying death.

Sigmund's terrible initial bout with cancer occurred at the same time as little Heinerle's death, which devastated Sigmund, plunging him into a deep depression. Sigmund lost all desire to go on after this, claiming his own health problems were of no consequence whatsoever. Later, he confided to one of his friends that from that point on he was completely unable to enjoy life, which may have explained his indifference to the medical danger that hovered over him. I question the validity of these thoughts. Did Heinerle's death mean more to him than that of his daughter Sophie? He did adore the little boy, that I know. And maybe Heinerle represented a little Sophie for him. She wasn't completely gone with him around. Or did Sigmund's own serious illness make this conclusion more eloquent?

It was at that time that Sigmund's mortality first became a reality for me, and all the repressed recriminations, small or large, I might have harbored evaporated into thin air. The suffering in Sigmund's sad face, with his horribly wounded mouth, broke my heart, overwhelming me with both pity and sorrow. How I longed to make him feel better, to be the one next to him. My sole desire was to help him through these terrible days. Such was not to be, however. From the beginning it had been decided between Anna and her father that she would play the role of nurse. I slept in the twin bed next to him, merely a night nurse. All that was left me was to help as best I could with his daily comfort. Access to my husband, such as I had enjoyed, was in effect denied me from that moment on, except through Anna, and with her permission. With admirable competence and courage, she made the medical decisions. I must have sunk into some kind of deep depression to have ever allowed my role to be taken over, without a shadow of protest.

Despite his declining health, Sigmund insisted on resuming his yearly summer vacation. With Dr. Hajek's blessings, in July he went to Bad Gastein, accompanied by Minna, after which he joined us in Lavrone for our normal family vacation. During a visit from Felix Deutch, it was discovered that a second tumor had appeared. Deutch ordered a second surgical procedure—this time in the hands of the eminent Professor Pichler, a renowned surgeon. The surgery was scheduled for October. The hope was that it would remove all malignant tissue. In the course of that second operation, it was discovered that Sigmund's hard palate had to be removed, thus making it necessary to implant a prosthesis that would enable Sigmund to speak and feed himself. Placing the prosthesis, which we had named with questionable humor "the monster," was no small challenge, and provoked tremendous pain for poor Sigmund. Anna, in charge of the process, managed heroically, often seeking a doctor's help.

Perturbed, and upset by what was happening to Sigmund, Minna like me, was suffering the humiliation of being shunted aside at this critical time. Her way of reacting was to raise her voice and dispatch orders to the domestics.

She rushed to answer the phone as soon as she heard it ringing; I once caught her saying, "Mrs. Freud speaking!" I let it pass. Why quarrel with the last remaining person in the house I had any rapport with? Years before, when she accompanied Sigmund to Bad Gastein, I am certain she had assumed the role of his wife. But those days were over. In any case, she was rarely with Sigmund anymore. Anna saw to that.

Most of Sigmund's daily activities had become labored and difficult. In fact, cancer had transformed him into a baby, for whom each of us had an assigned maternal role. For one, his speech had become almost incomprehensible, so he tended not to speak. Sigi chewed with difficulty, and most of the time Anna was there to help him through his meals. Moreover, the trumpet that had been placed in his ear had become damaged, which exasperated the infection localized not far away, making him more deaf than before. The position of his conch had to be artfully changed so he could hear his patients.

As extraordinary as it may seem, given the circumstances, Sigmund continued working. His patients kept multiplying, and he continued to write whenever he felt up to it until his death. One must remember that starting not long after the end of World War I, Sigmund had become a worldwide celebrity. Psychoanalysis was fast becoming recognized globally, and Sigmund's writings were being published everywhere, especially in France, after the famous French writer André Gide asked permission to publish some of his works in the prestigious literary review *La Nouvelle Revue Française*. Sigmund was receiving mountains of admiring letters every day from around the world, all of which helped his morale.

Everyone had assumed that the onset of Sigmund's illness and Heinerle's death were the elements that first triggered his preoccupation with death. Wrong. Later, Ferenczi told me that as far back as 1921 Sigmund's obsession on the subject had begun, and that he had engaged in a long dialogue about it with him. Minna reminded me that as far back as 1920 Sigmund had already published a text, *Beyond the Pleasure Principle*, whose focus was death, which apparently had raised quite a storm with his pupils. In it Sigmund questioned one of psychoanalysis's fundamental theories, which claimed Eros as the force behind everything, aggression being one of its manifestations. Sigmund introduced the notion of Thanatos, which he claimed was as deeply embedded in the human psyche, thus undermining Eros's work. According to Sigmund, this was the only way of understanding man's self-destructive powers, as well as his destructive powers against his fellow man. Sigmund's research on war neuroses had apparently furnished him with plenty of food for thought. How else could one understand the necessity for man to relive trauma? What about nightmares? Why did man feel endlessly compelled to destroy what he had built? This new formula was in total contradiction to the optimistic position formulated in his earlier theories, and was poorly received. Jones was the first to tell Sigmund he was far from convinced, calling the notion speculative and bordering on the nonsensical, with a tendency to mystical depravation, which was the supreme condemnation. Despite his protestations to the contrary, most people agreed that Sigmund's thinking had been influenced by his personal losses, especially those of Sophie and Heinerle.

While I had never involved myself in Sigmund's theo-retical work, his reflections on death both troubled and touched me greatly. There were deeper meanings to his recent presentation. Although I accepted his theory on sexuality, I found it simplistic at times. The notion of mysticism, on the other hand, even though I had abandoned any kind of religious life, did touch upon something that secretly always fascinated me—the element beyond human reason. I wondered whether Sigmund had not introduced a new dimension to psychoanalysis, accepting the notion of the unknown, the unknowable. Although Sigmund insisted in keeping within the boundaries of science, wasn't he, with his new theory, touching upon precisely what constituted the mystical, or what religion was trying to do? This may explain why some of his most rationalistic students vehemently opposed his theory. Perhaps that is why he felt obliged to defend himself by launching even stronger attacks against the citadel of religion. Perhaps, too, he was facing up to something he had always refused to admit, namely that psychoanalysis, his creation, had its limits. Wasn't Sigi bumping against the walls, the limits of psychoanalysis?

I was reminded of a quotation from Goethe's *Faust*, which Sigmund had borrowed to illustrate a point in a letter to Stefan Zweig that I had recently come upon. Relating to Joseph F. Breuer's fleeing after learning of Bertha Pappenheim's made-up pregnancy, he wrote: "He held in his hands the keys that would have opened The Doors to the Mothers, but he dropped them. Despite his many talents, there was nothing Faustian about him." Goethe has always been among my favorite authors. I have read and reread *Faust* many times, and this quote was not unfamiliar to me. I found the place with the reference to these enigmatic "Doors to the Mothers." It happens in the second part of *Faust*, when Mephistopheles evokes the goddesses capable of making Helen and Paris appear.

> Solemnly, the goddesses sit enthroned in solitary splendor. Around them, neither place nor, even more so, time. To speak of them is disconcerting. They are the Mothers.

As Faust asks what direction he should take to find them, he is answered:

> No clear path! It is in the mind, where no one can make his way; a path toward the undesired, toward the inaccessible. Are you ready? Neither locks to open nor bolts to slide back; you will wander amidst not one but many lonelinesses. Have you any idea of the void, of loneliness?

I have always been awed by this text, with its admirable poetic language. What is most moving to me is how Goethe creates an echo of mystery, of the unknown, evoking a hidden place where the ultimate explanation to man's confrontation with his enigmas lies. A mystical text, most certainly. Seeing my husband—the notorious atheist, the great rationalist—refer to that text surprised me greatly. But I had dismissed it at the time as one more of Sigmund's literary references.

Today, however, I am not so sure. If Breuer was not Faustian, Sigmund, I am convinced, must have wanted to be so. Very young, he had pictured himself as conqueror—often referring to himself as a "conquistador"—a man capable of confronting dangers and discovering new territories. He really became one, didn't he? Wasn't Sigmund the intrepid hero who, after surmounting every obstacle, discovered the secrets hidden in the depth of the human being? Wasn't he the one, like Oedipus, to solve the Sphinx's enigma? Didn't Sigmund fight against and conquer his own demons, overcome anxieties, against all odds, to finally arrive at a place where no one had ever gone before? He did indeed throw down a huge challenge to the established order, to the moralizing fathers, to God himself, and, like all those who found anything new, did it not place him above all the other men, leading him, as the poet says "to roam in the realm of solitude"?

At a certain moment in his life, Sigmund had reached a point where the unbeaten track, the undesired, the inaccessible, was worrying him more than the mysteries of the unconscious. It had no longer to do with the mysteries of sexuality—rather insignificant, after all. It was addressing the larger mystery, the one man confronts when faced with death. And, for the first time, I will confess to being in total harmony and accord with Sigmund's research.

Dear Mary, you see where my digressions lead me. Still, I am pleased to have been able to confide in you, rambling though I was.

So much more to say. But later.

Martha F.

16

How I envy Anna, writes Mary in her letter. The closeness with her father, the love Anna enjoyed her entire life, was what Mary had missed terribly. Poor dear. She of course doesn't realize that Anna's lot was not much more enviable than hers. Mary at least, forced to liberate herself, lived her life, even at the cost of sufferings. That was denied my youngest daughter.

The day I caught in one glimpse the full negative brunt of our family structure—that New Year's day family reunion in 1923, with Sigmund surrounded by his mother, sisters, daughters, his grandson on his lap, forming a perfect family scene Greuze would have loved to paint—I also saw signs of death. Death? Death from suffocation, from a glue that stuck them together around their irreplaceable and unique father. That glue, as I perceived it then, was the very instrument of their destruction. As I watched Sigmund's almighty mother, the full meaning of incest—so central to Sigmund's work— struck me that day, as well. How is it that I, who was part of that circle of Sigmund women, was the one to perceive the meaning of this tableau?

Hard to say. Could it be that I had simply used up all my inner reserves, and was no longer capable of enduring the rivalries, the abandonment? I had stepped outside the tableau. Anyway, as his wife, did I really belong in that tableau? Sigmund had made me a mother. I was the only one present to have shared his bed, which helped distance me from it all, a little like the statutes of an outsider.

Does anyone know that Anna had been analyzed by her own father? It began in 1918, when Anna decided to become an analyst. I reassured myself at the time that Sigmund was no doubt doing this to help and further her career. As the analysis progressed, however, I began to wonder. Anna lived practically every minute of each day with Sigmund, shared his work in ways few colleagues had been privileged to. Now, to top it off, she was confiding personal secrets, her most shameful thoughts—the very kind people never reveal to anyone except to their analyst, with whom presumably there is no interaction in life. This, I realize, was sealing her life to his forever. In 1919 Sigmund published an article with the title "A Child Is Beaten." In 1922 Anna gave a lecture in Berlin on the same subject. At this point, Anna did not yet have any patients. The subject of her lecture—incestuous phantasm between a father and his daughter—had a rather obvious autobiographical tone, which did not escape the notice of the audience. Did she do this to defy the critics? Or were they both so blind as to ignore what the world would judge highly objectionable? That is not all I find reprehensible. How could Sigmund have allowed this young woman—whose obsessive love for him was more than obvious—to be analyzed by him, thereby making sure to solidify their bond? Clearly, instead of her analyst becoming her liberator, in this case he tightened that very bond. Results speak for themselves: Anna never left her father. She became his collaborator, his voice in conferences, his spiritual executor, his nurse, closer to him than anyone else.

In 1925 Sigmund gave Anna a German shepherd,

whose mission was to protect her on her long walks. That dog, whose name was Wolf, played the role of child for them both. Wolf sat between them at dinner, and the intrusive complicity of those three became increasingly insufferable to me. The same went for the special friendship Anna struck up with Dorothy the same year. With subtlety, Sigmund made sure that that friendship would unfold near him. He had to be part of it, as he had been with Wolf, mixing friendship, family, and psychoanalysis. All boundaries became blurred, and no matter what Anna's new interest was, so long as she indulged it in Sigmund's close proximity, it was fine.

Did Anna benefit from this special situation? Of course. There is no question but that her father's name did help her career, especially after he officially anointed her in the eyes of the world. Is she worthy of having been granted this responsibility or destiny? Undoubtedly. But her total and blatant identification with her father borders on fraud, in my opinion. Of course, Anna is extremely intelligent. Her work reveals intense labor, but without particular spark. As far as children's analysis is concerned—from which she derives full glory, as its founder—I find her rival Melanie Klein's work far more interesting. Melanie doesn't limit her craft to a superficial pedagogy tainted with psychoanalysis. All Anna is really doing is applying her father's theories. Doesn't she realize this?

Alienated, sterile, Anna is the product of her father, displaying the strength of her own desire. In an effort to underline her heroism vis-à-vis him, Sigmund used to call her his Antigone. Didn't the name—Antigone, daughter of Oedipus—reveal their incestuous relationship? How is it that the inventor of the tool for freeing people's psyches could not apply it to himself? I guess he could not explore much further. A pity he could not experiment more deeply with one of his students. It was no doubt impossible. To them Sigmund was a living god. The worship his students had for him came to a head when Sigmund became ill with cancer. They were terrified of losing him. It would also have required, on his part, a humility that, frankly, was foreign to him. Sigmund hung on to his status as the father of psychoanalysis—a father who could not tolerate the idea of having someone above him.

17

Dear Mary,

You ask that I describe what followed. If only you knew how little I wish to talk about these last years! Vienna, and Sigmund's last years, were depressing. Life had become dark, punctuated only by the many operations Sigmund's cancer necessitated. Everyone was going around with a long face.

While gloom permeated our home life, renewed energy had returned to Vienna, under the Social Democratic government. Large communities erected for workers, who for the first time lived under decent conditions, were troubling the middle class. The threat of Bolshevism was beginning to be heard. Two militia sprung up: a conservative militia, the Heimwehren, and the Schutzbunde, the Social Democrats. From 1927 on these two factions confronted each other daily, creating an ongoing feeling of insecurity in the city. It came to a head on July 15 of that year, when a huge throng of hundreds of thousands marched on the Ring to protest the liberation from prison of three members of the Heimwehr, who were accused of killing three workers. The mob, in a paroxysm of anger, set the Palace of Justice building on fire, leaving eighty-two dead. When in 1930 the Karl-Marx-Hof—a huge compound built like a fortress—was completed, anxiety was on every moderate person's mind.

The country had entered a period of political unrest, exacerbated by the economic depression. The effect of the 1929 crash of the New York Stock Exchange had reached Europe. Our son Martin, who worked in a bank, was filling our ears with dreadful tales of panic, with people committing suicide right and left, and men throwing themselves off of skyscrapers. All of this had repercussions in Vienna, of course. Banks went under. People lost their jobs from one day to the next. Unemployment rose each day.

In a curious act of fate, we Freuds were spared much of this crisis, due in great part to the increasing number of wealthy foreign patients knocking on my husband's door over the course of the decade. Sigmund had also wisely invested some money in Switzerland, which in later years was to be a godsend. Still, we could not be unaware of the pervasive climate of insecurity all around us.

In 1930 Sigmund was awarded the Goethe Prize—a prize of enormous prestige, which provoked an enthusiastic response as messages of congratulations flooded in. But somehow Sigmund wasn't particularly happy about it, feeling he had been awarded the prize for the wrong reasons. What was more, he was rather depressed. His most precious pupils had left him. Abraham had died. Rank and Ferenczi held him at a distance. He was surrounded by females. Many of his women patients became his friends, the most important of whom was Marie Bonaparte. Many of his women patients were referred to him by Anna. What a change for Sigmund, a man whose male professional relationships had meant so much to him! From that time on, his entourage consisted of women, all vying for his exclusive attention.

From 1930 on, social troubles were on the rise, and the Social Democrats quickly lost power. By 1932 the Austrian Nazis were the third largest party in the capital. On January 30, 1933, Hitler took power in Berlin. Three months later, the Dollfuss government dissolved the parliament, as well as the Schutzbunde, the Social Democrat militia.

Despite our preoccupation with Sigmund's illness, we could not remain indifferent to what was unfolding in the outside world. Both Ernst and Oliver immediately left Berlin, as did a large number of Jews who had awakened to the fact that their German nationality would not serve them. Hitler couldn't have been clearer: Jewish vermin would be eliminated by every means possible.

Psychoanalysis was the first hit. Most Jewish members of the Psychoanalytical Society handed in their resignation, believing they were saving their cause. With the Nazis, however, no compromise existed. Under Dr. Göring's supervision, that institution became Aryanized, and deviated from its goals. Psychoanalysis was finished; Göring would see to it personally.

I find it difficult to believe that Sigmund could have believed that all this affected only Germany, that Austria would be spared. It was the same when, back in 1914, his books were all burned. I remember him saying, "It could be worse! In the Middle Ages, they would have burned me as well!" From these fires to the crematoriums of later years . . . Everyone was pressing Sigmund to emigrate, not to wait till the plague reached Austria. "Nonsense!" he would repeat endlessly, as he had in the past. He was convinced that the high level of civilization in Austria would prevent barbaric German behavior from happening there.

The world as I had known it was collapsing. Terrified and in shock, I was unable to grasp the situation; I couldn't fathom that what had been my secure environment, a culture of which I felt an integral part, was all of a sudden pushing us out. How did I not see it coming? Had the Germans around us always hated us? Under the influence of that demonic man, did Germany unleash its demons?

Nineteen-thirty-four was a frightful year. In February, militant Socialists and armed police entered into fierce combat, and the suburbs resembled hastily erected fortresses to which people fled in droves. One by one these fortresses collapsed—the last to fall, symbolically, was Karl-Marx-Hof. In this short civil war, the Socialists were defeated, there were countless dead, and the Social Democratic Party was abolished. Town hall fell into the hands of the Social Christian Party. The Red Vienna had survived only two weeks. As things fell back into some semblance of order, people bemoaned the loss of the Hapsburg Empire, when Austria was still big and powerful. I remember back in 1932 reading *The Radetzky March*, in which the author, Joseph Roth, set modern mediocrity, with the growing barbaric influence emanating from Germany, against the past, blissful empire. I found myself nostalgic as well for the good old days of monarchy, when our good emperor had protected us all. Revolutionary speeches had a way of scaring me. As for Sigmund, he seemed in favor of some moderate liberalism.

In July, Austrian Nazis attempted a putsch that failed, but cost Chancellor Dollfuss his life. It took less than four years for Hitler to impose on Dollfuss's successor, Kurt von Schuschnigg, his plan of annexing Austria to Germany. National Socialism was in control.

Everything was obviously closing in on us. It was already clear that Nazi ideology, with its thematic barbarism, saw us as prime targets. No! Sigmund continued to say, he would not leave. He would not desert. Why? Did he think he was captain of a ship, the general of an army? Was he so prideful that he saw himself a hero, that he thought his sacrifice had some symbolic value? A childish challenge, I thought. David against Goliath. Or did Sigmund feel his name alone would protect us?

During this time, Sigmund, paler and each day more fragile, continued writing between each operation. In the course of that terrible and decisive year, 1934, Sigmund edited his work *Moses and Monotheism,* which was published in England. I saw Sigmund reading the Bible. In his last two books, *The Future of an Illusion* and *Civilization and Its Discontents,* he never stopped condemning religion, declaring it a consoling drug—the illusion rocking the individual to sleep—and clearly stating his atheism. He was pitting science against some childish pipe dream, insisting that science, if not infallible, at least paved the way for adult reasoning. Could the growing anti-Semitism have made him question his condition as a Jew? No. I realized that this had nothing to do with it.

When I finally read *Moses and Monotheism,* it both surprised and shocked me. Sigmund's Moses was no longer a Hebrew prince, as I'd always thought, but an Egyptian one. According to Sigmund, Moses was an adept of a monotheism founded by Akhenaten in the fourteenth century before Christ, who had been obliged to flee Egypt when the priests of the old religion revolted and reinstated the old religion. Moses, according to Sigmund, would have chosen his people from among the slaves living in the far reaches of the empire, and imposed his laws upon them. They in turn, wanting nothing to do with his laws, assassinated Moses. It was the horror of their crime, and the remorse that followed, that, according to Sigmund's new theory, gave rise to the Jewish religion with all its dictates.

Some twenty years before, Sigmund in his *Totem and Taboo* had already formulated a similar hypothesis, probing and explaining in a more general way the origin of religion. I recall not understanding, or sharing at the time, Sigmund's theory of the original murder, where the sons' guilt for the murder of the leader/father had imposed the necessity to found the cult on the very person they had murdered. At the time I had questioned Sigmund's historical hypothesis, which I found rather risky at best.

Why take away the foundations of their religion at a time when Jews were already threatened? Why remove Moses' Jewish status? Why? Whose truth was it, anyway? I was deeply troubled. For me, no matter what Sigmund's theories might be, for me Moses incarnated our father, who had led the oppressed Jews out of slavery. The wonderful Seder and Pesach meals that reunited our family, celebrating that essential page of our history, came flooding back to me with nostalgia: my father, who each time questioned: "What makes this evening different from the others?" The poetry of the occasion, and our being assembled together around our table, gave each of us strength. Why deprive us of that?

Didn't Sigmund resolve rather high-handedly questions posed by man since time immemorial? Wasn't his notion—that God was the infantile image of a father who had to be eliminated—absurd? These were the questions and conjectures I wrestled with in those days. But I decided to keep it all to myself.

At the time, Sigmund's writings made me not only unhappy but irritated with him. I simply did not understand him. Reading on, I came to the conclusion that his perception of the Supreme Being was of someone mirroring his own image. Sigmund too had combated injustice, treason. He too had been rejected by those close to him. None of this consoled me. I found it, to the contrary, preposterous, and resented that he was solely concerned with his own image at a historical moment when so much more important and serious trouble was facing us.

Why make Moses a goy? Did Moses, as a non-Jew, place Sigmund in a different category from his fellow Jews, preventing him from submitting to a religion, but giving him the right to found his own? Did everything always have to do with putting himself first? In school! The firstborn! First in his mother's heart! In science! Always leading the pack! But, I wondered, wasn't there more than a little folly in always wanting to be first in everything?

Sigmund must have had his own doubts about this text, for he postponed publication. The book was published shortly before he died. Even then, I recall wishing he had kept it all secret. That book exposed Sigmund's less estimable side, which I greatly regretted. But given all he had endured—exile, illness—who was I to judge or reproach him?

*   *   *

My husband's relationship with Judaism—his father's religion—had always been violent. When I met Sigmund, his aversion to anything to do with religion reflected an attitude I thought purely philosophical, atheism being much in vogue among his generation. But with him, I felt it took on far greater significance. Throughout our engagement, his attempt to wrench me from religious superstitions was obsessive, at the forefront of Sigmund's preoccupations. It had been decided that we would marry in Wandsbeck, because in Germany, as opposed to Austria, religious weddings were not obligatory—a decision that was reversed when we learned that Austria would not recognize a civil marriage. With great reluctance and a heavy heart Sigmund finally resigned himself to learning a few Hebrew formulas and coming to the synagogue with his head covered and a prayer shawl over his shoulders. I never saw this again.

Deep down, I blessed this legal problem. I would have been very unhappy had we been deprived of the wedding ceremony that, in my eyes, was so important. Much later, and to my utter shock, I learned that in the light of our legal problem in trying to avoid a Jewish ceremony, Sigmund had been ready to embrace Protestantism. Only Joseph Breuer's influence ultimately dissuaded him. We never spoke about it. In any case, all religious conversations became taboo in our house on the first Friday after our honeymoon. As I was about to light the candles to celebrate the Sabbath, Sigmund took the candelabra from my hands and, in a solemn tone, ordered me never to do that again! I was thunderstruck, and my eyes filled with tears. Pointless tears—I never had the strength to resist him.

From then on—and I still question how I accepted this—I gave up for good my ancestors' religion. There are those who, like Anna, maintain that I abandoned one religion for another—that of believing in Sigmund. "My mother never believed in psychoanalysis," was how she put it; "she only believed in my father." No doubt true for most of my life. She doesn't know, however, that this is no longer true. On the contrary. In fact, the Friday following Sigmund's death, I lit a candle and found myself back in the Sabbath ritual of my youth, which I have since repeated each Friday ever since. It only took fifty-three years to allow myself this. Isn't it shameful? Inexcusable? For over half a century I had accepted Sigmund's word on the most important things in exchange for his love. A fool's pact, no? Today, I find myself angry as much at myself as at him.

On another subject, did you know, dear Mary, that after endless procrastination Sigmund finally, on June 4, 1938, agreed to leave his Vienna? It was high time. I am in no mood to write about all this in detail. The memory is too close, and too painful.

I suspect, in fact, that this is going to be my last letter. I am, thanks to you, freed of my own story. To no one else will I tell it. I can now finish my days with dignity. I have more than enough food for thought to fill my last days, my last months, my last years, if it comes to that. For the past year I have reflected on all that happened during this last war. People are rebuilding, saying, "This will never happen again!" Quite normal, I understand. The world is celebrating peace—singing, dancing, giving birth to a new generation. But I can't imagine the world escaping without profound scars. I am not alone, I know, in thinking that an era that has experienced genocide with perfect methodology, systematically on the basis of a mad rationale, will leave man vulnerable forever. There will be no place where one can feel safe from fanaticism and deadly folly.

Please forgive my pessimistic way of concluding our correspondence. From the start of our dialogue, I vowed to be totally sincere. It is with relief that I know that whatever I have written you—including my last thoughts—will evaporate into nothingness. It must make room for something else. As for me, I am pleased to be able, in the time left to me, to ponder some fundamental questions. My questions.

Mary, I can't thank you enough for having allowed me to travel on this journey of self-discovery, where I have learned so much. Without you, I'm sure it would not have been possible.

Take care,

Martha F.

18

I couldn't share with Mary what had been gnawing at me for several months as I wrote her that final letter — a thought so painful and violent I could not bring myself to mention it to her. Besides, to whom could I confide it without opening a can of worms? Neither Sigmund nor Minna ever learned what happened to Sigmund's four sisters in 1942. I only found out myself this past year during the Nuremberg trials. Yes, as we suspected, they had been arrested, but we had no notion of what that meant exactly. Whenever I think about it, I cringe in horror and unbearable shame.

Rosa, Mitzi, Dolfi, Pauli. My good friends of Kaiser-Josefstrasse; so trusting, so naïve, so dependent on one another, so totally under their brother's spell. I remember, when he was still an adolescent, Sigmund joking that he and his brother Alexander formed the binding of a book whose pages were his sisters. Did he mean by that that he would protect them? I translated this as being more like those two brothers representing the German shepherds, keeping the sheep on the straight and narrow. The only one who survived was Anna. Tough Anna, Anna who dreamed only of leaving her siblings behind, starting with her brother, the place he held in her mother's heart, her mother who had never loved her. She alone had the courage to leave everything: the Freuds, Vienna, old Europe, where the worst was brewing in the hearts and minds of evil men. Ultimately that is what saved her life.

The four remaining sisters had had a difficult life. Not much was left after the young god had taken his share. It was almost a given for the sisters to be left with a mediocre existence. There were in fact only two people in the Freud family, Sigmund and his mother, whom heaven had chosen to favor.

Once widowed, all the sisters joined forces and went to live in the same small apartment. It's hard for me to go on. . . . Anyway, in 1938 Princess Bonaparte, with the help of the American ambassador to France, W. C. Bullit, obtained favorable conditions for our departure. We were offered the ability to bring with us those we deemed important. When it came time to make a decision about Sigmund's sisters, he insisted that once he was in England, he would not have the wherewithal to support them. It was best to give them a good sum of money and leave them in Vienna. What could Sigmund have been thinking? That their advanced age would save them from the fate overhanging all Austria's Jews? That they would be spared because of his famous name?

On June 4, 1938, Sigmund, Anna, Paula, and I left Vienna. Minna had preceded us. Martin was coming as well, with his wife, and so was Mathilde, her husband, and their maid. We had obtained a visa for Sigmund's doctor, Max Schur, who at the last minute had to stay behind because of an appendicitis attack. A friend of Anna's, Dr. Josephine Stross, came in his place to take care of Sigmund during the crossing. We were fifteen in all. Could we not have been nineteen just as well? The sisters were left behind, waiting for their executioner.

In 1940 I received through the Red Cross a card from

Rosa telling me how sad and lonely they were. In 1942, all four were arrested and sent to Theresienstadt. Dolfi died of starvation in 1943. Rosa was gassed in Treblinka; Mitzi and Pauli disappeared in another camp, Maly Trostinec. I followed the Nuremberg trials, and thus was able to picture in my mind what these poor women had to endure: terror, humiliation, cold, hunger, death under the most atrocious circumstances. As for the protection the Freud name provided them, I knew, from reading the minutes of the trial, what had happened to Rosa. She, having arrived in the camp after her horrifying voyage there, ran toward a Nazi officer, telling him she was Professor Freud's sister. He replied, taking her by the arm, "Of course. This must be a mistake. Follow me!" and led her into the gas chamber.

I am tortured by all this, and I only regret that Sigmund never knew. What was wrong with me? How could I have remained so passive, and not insisted on having Sigmund's sisters come with the rest of us? If there was one day when I could have shown my true colors, this was the one. And I failed miserably.

I can't go on; my heart is too heavy and filled with anger. I get up, walk over to the window, and gaze outside. It is raining now, an icy drizzle that covers the windowpanes with a gray veil. I sit down in front of the abandoned jigsaw puzzle but am incapable of even looking at, much less making any sense out of, the jumble of pieces, so filled is my mind with frightful thoughts. There was no way we couldn't have known what the Nazis were up to. How in the world did Sigmund ever for a minute believe that he was above the law and would be spared the fate of all the other Jews? Nineteen thirty-three had sounded the death knell of all our illusions.

Ernst and Oliver knew what was up, and both immediately
left Berlin—Ernst for England, Oliver for France. How
many other Jewish intellectuals, including many famous
ones, quickly followed suit! Sigmund knew full well that his
books had been burned. In 1938 we had witnessed two hundred thousand jubilant Black Shirts marching to welcome
Hitler after having beaten a Jew and forcing him to get on his
knees to brush the pavement for the victory parade.

We kept our heads high, though, when a few days later
five horrible SS soldiers burst into our apartment, demanding money. I received them with the courtesy of a hostess,
inviting them to sit down, went to fetch some money, and,
shaking like a leaf, handed them six thousand shillings,
which took them somewhat aback. Undoubtedly, they had
expected to find elderly people scared to death and were already reveling in the prospect. But my courtliness did not
prevent them from scooping up all sorts of personal items. As
they were in the midst of their thievery, Sigmund burst out of
his office and stared them down, at which point they took the
money and left.

Dr. Jones was in Vienna and insisted that we emigrate as
soon as possible. "There is no time to waste!" he urged us. To
which Sigmund would respond, "I'm too weak to travel!" or
"No country would grant me asylum!" or above all—the real
reason—"How could I leave my country at a time like this?"
What finally won the day was that Anna's future was in danger. Finally, he agreed to leave. It was almost too late. For-
malities would take time, and in no way were we secure
during the waiting period.

A week later, as it turned out, men from the Gestapo arrived armed, this time with dogs in tow. Once again they

searched our apartment, demanding money, papers, Lord knows what. I led them to our safe, and once more, they helped themselves. These dark men of ice were terrifying in their long leather coats and soft hats. Then they demanded that Sigmund follow them to the Psychoanalytical Society. Anna interceded, saying she would go in his place.

They kept her all day. Sigmund was sick with anxiety, fearing she would be tortured. Gritting his teeth, he paced the floor like a caged lion. Paula went several times to the Society, seeking news, to no avail. Anna finally returned at seven that evening, pale and shaking so she could barely speak. They had let her go thanks to the intervention of Dorothy, who alerted the American embassy. That final incident was the straw that broke the camel's back for Sigmund. They had frightened and threatened his precious child, her whom he cherished most in the world, and that was intolerable. Each of us spent the following days waiting with anxiety for the exit visas to come through. Minna and I spent the time busy folding linen and packing clothes. Anna and Marie Bonaparte were going through Sigmund's books, determining which should be sold and which we should take. Sigmund was poring over his papers.

Finally on June 4, we left the country.

I remember all that followed as if in a dream, one of those dreams in which one is a spectator, incapable of taking part in what is going on. I went about everything passively, silently. At no time was I asked my opinion. All major decisions were made by others. Although it seemed normal at the time, it troubles me to look back at the inert human being I then was. Have I changed? I don't know, for I am desperately trying to comprehend why I never bothered thinking for my-self, deciding my own fate, why my entire existence was fo-cused on someone else's life. I think of all the women who, for the sake of someone they love, relinquish all their rights. Is that love, this gift of one's self?

So many questions I must address, so many enigmas to confront. That's all that concerns me these days, however many may still be granted me.

19

Dear Mary,

Imagine my surprise, dear Mary, upon learning of the birth
of your daughter! I send you my warmest congratulations!
You named her Martha, which touches me deeply. That you
wanted to have a child—during the course of our long
correspondence I had been under the impression that becoming a mother was the last thing you contemplated—both
surprises and mystifies me, but in no way lessens my joy
for you.

I have the feeling that most of my letters have conveyed
doom and gloom, and my own sense of the end of life. How
wrong! I guess one can never judge what one imparts when
one opens the doors to what had been closed for so long.
Since the end of our letter writing, I think of you often—as a
daughter.

I can't describe to you how precious our epistolary relationship has been for me. How much it has brought me. And
how much I thank you for it.

I spent all of the summer in my garden. These past few
weeks I have been enjoying the splendor of the summer's last
roses. I've been reading Shakespeare, with dictionary in

hand, to be sure. Poets are the only ones reconciling me to the human species. Perhaps I may find other resources to reconcile me further.

I am well. A bit slower, more tired. I use the elevator now to go upstairs, and venture outside the house but rarely.

But I feel at peace, ready for the end. But not impatiently—there are still so many books I have to read.

I send you my fond embrace,

Martha F.

20

Last night, I finally put the last piece of the jigsaw puzzle into place. The painting is finally finished, brilliant under the overhead light. Perfect. And yet, now that it's done, I don't have the feeling of satisfaction I was expecting; why, I don't know. I'm contemplating undoing it and putting all the pieces back in the box.

Lucy offered me another puzzle for my last birthday, one that depicts a naval battle, full of exquisite details, which promises me many hours bent over my table trying to figure out where this or that piece should go.

Somehow I can't bring myself to take the new puzzle out of its box. Maybe lack of desire. Maybe having just completed one, I have a feeling I've done what I set out to do and don't need another such challenge.

But who knows? I'm going to carefully keep this gift in some special place, assuming that one day I may feel the need for it. One never knows.

Postface

Whenever Martha is referred to in any of Freud's biographies, she is described in the same way. They all mention the passion that she inspired in him, the proof of which is the thousand letters he wrote her during the four years they were engaged. But in contrast to that richly documented period, a scant few lines are all that describe—or dismiss—the fifty-three years of their marriage. Ernest Jones's lines, in a kind of epitaph to Martha when she died in 1951, epitomize this tendency: "Few unions were as happy as theirs. Martha, an excellent mother, an excellent wife, belonged to that rare breed of fine housewives able to keep their domestics indefinitely. Her husband's comfort and well-being took priority over everything else." Since in addition it appears that this woman reputedly showed little or no interest in her husband's work, she was quickly relegated to the background, a discreet but indispensable figure in her husband's entourage, to the point of virtually disappearing altogether.

That portrait always surprised and, I have to confess, revolted me. One can well understand that Freud was more than satisfied with a wife entirely devoted to his well-being. He had other people with whom to exchange ideas and theories. But what about Martha? Was this woman stupid enough throughout her life not only to have accepted a purely domestic role but to have remained oblivious, indifferent, to the work of the man she shared her life with—

whose work revolutionized modern thinking? Could her role have satisfied her as fully as people were wont to say? What is more, despite the singular discretion with which these shadowy zones are alluded to, that they did nonetheless exist remains obvious. Documents reveal that, beyond her Germanic stiffness, Martha was not only a cultivated woman but one capable of humor. How and why, then, could she have agreed to remain in the background and devote her life to serving her husband?

My answers to these questions could only come in the form of a novel, if only because I wanted Martha to express herself in the first person. I therefore created a fictional character, Mrs. Huntington-Smith, whom I cast as her sympathetic correspondent. I imagined Martha—age eighty-five, seven years after her husband's death—not only retracing her life but questioning much of it, while at the same time reexamining the golden legend created around the inventor of psychoanalysis. I wanted to enable Martha to emerge from obscurity, to assert her own person-ality; I wanted to make her three-dimensional for the first time. In other words, give her a voice.

I take full responsibility for Martha's writings, thoughts, and the scenes that spring entirely from my imagination. At the same time, this fiction is so closely related to and intertwined with reality that what I created rings just as true to me as the facts on which they are based. It is the real Martha who appears, as depicted in the archival documents of the Freud family. I have invented nothing regarding Martha's background, historical context, or the personalities of any of the characters, including their physical descriptions, in any way differently from the sources over which I pored. The historical and personal events they lived through can, alas, be verified. The interested reader can find these sources in the following volumes:

The first monumental volume of Freud's biography, by Ernest Jones, was published in New York in 1953, barely two years after Martha's death, and is entitled *The Life and Work of Sigmund Freud.*

In 1991, a more modern biography appeared, Peter Gay's *A Life of Our Time,* less dense, more accessible, a little impertinent. But again, as in the previous biography, Martha occupies little space.

The first biography dedicated solely to Martha was published in Germany in 2002 by Aufbau Taschenbuch Verlag: *Martha Freud: Die Frau des Genie,* by Katja Behling, with a preface by Anton Freud, Martin's son. Perfectly documented, it is as respectful of the Freudian hagiography as the other books on Freud, giving Martha the same treatment. More recently, in *The Dictionary of Psychoanalysis,* edited by Elizabeth Rodinesco and Michel Plon, and in Alain de Mijolla's *International Dictionary of Psychoanalysis,* one can find well-documented articles on all members of the Freud family and on the other characters who appear in this book.

Freud's correspondence is also of enormous interest. In particular, the few letters to Martha not locked up in the Library of Congress, in Washington, D.C., can be found in *Sigmund Freud's Correspondence, 1873–1939.* As for the William Fliess and Sigmund Freud relationship, my sources were *The Birth of Psychoanalysis, Letters to Wilhelm Fliess* and the two volumes of Freud's exchanges with Carl Gustav Jung, *The Freud/Jung Letters: 1906–1909* and *1910–1914*, published in 1979.

There are many anecdotes in Martin Freud's book *Freud, My Father*, published in 1989 in New York, as well as in *The Freud Family, Day to Day*, by Detlef Berthelsen, published in Munich in 1989.

To actually view the historical settings of this story, I recommend the book of photographs that Ernst Freud, Lucie Freud, and Ilse Gruber-Simitis assembled, *Sigmund Freud: Places, Faces, Objects*, which Gallimard published in France in 1979. Contemplating this family album has been invaluable for me, a source of rich inspiration.